HELL ON HOOFS

Arriving in Lancerville, John Laramie hoped to escape his old life as a man-hunter and settle down. But there he finds he's torn between the demons of his past and hope for a brighter future when a young woman seeks his help in getting rid of a vicious outlaw. Then the Cross Gang attacks him and the young woman's life is put in danger. But will it cost Laramie more to win than to lose in a deadly showdown?

Books by Lance Howard
in the Linford Western Library:

THE COMANCHE'S GHOST
THE WEST WITCH
THE GALLOWS GHOST
THE WIDOW MAKER
GUNS OF THE PAST
PALOMITA
THE LAST DRAW
THE DEADLY DOVES
WANTED
THE DEVIL'S PEACEMAKER
THE WEST WOLF
THE PHANTOM MARSHAL
BANDOLERO
PIRATE PASS
THE SILVER-MINE SPOOK
NIGHTMARE PASS
HELL PASS
BLOOD CREEK
THE DEVIL'S RIDER
COYOTE DEADLY
DEAD MAN RIDING
THE KILLING KIND

LANCE HOWARD

HELL ON HOOFS

Complete and Unabridged

LINFORD
Leicester

First published in Great Britain in 2011 by
Robert Hale Limited
London

First Linford Edition
published 2013
by arrangement with
Robert Hale Limited
London

A catalogue record for this book is available
from the British Library.

ISBN 978–1–4448–1635–8

Published by
F. A. Thorpe (Publishing)
Anstey, Leicestershire

For Tannenbaum

*Please visit Lance Howard
on the web at
www.howardhopkins.com*

1

Too many times lately the ghosts from John Laramie's nightmares haunted his waking hours and poisoned his veins with guilt. Images seeped from his dark dreams: blood streaming down hard merciless faces, the specter of death frozen in widened eyes that stared sightlessly at nothing. Dead men, all by his hand.

Along with the images, sounds roared through his brain: the screams and cries for mercy that never came, the echoes of his own withering conscience, which pleaded with him that enough was enough. Too much killing, too much blood on his hands, and on his soul. Morally justified killings, but killings nonetheless.

Some outlaws went with spite or hate or contempt on their features; others went with fear. But they all went. That was the constant.

Hunched at a table in the Lancerville saloon, he raised the whiskey glass to his lips, let the amber liquor wash over his tongue and slide down his throat, burning. But it didn't burn enough to sear the guilt away, nor purge the darkness he had felt threatening to devour his soul for the past few years.

It was getting stronger, that darkness. Sometimes it damn near overwhelmed him. The darkness wanted him, entreated him, promised to turn him into a remorseless creature who delivered death for a price, and for a façade of justice.

That was why he had to quit. Before it was too late, if, indeed, he were not already beyond redemption.

He shook his head, wishing the whiskey would act faster, deaden his damning thoughts and plunging mood, but it was watered, and pitifully impotent. His gaze lifted, swept about the small saloon. Through a Durham haze he noted a couple men peering at him, perhaps recognizing the man the dime novels had dubbed 'Hell on Hoofs', perhaps wondering why the hell he was in their pissant nowhere town, and whether trouble had ridden in with him.

A nauseating jumble of odors assailed his nostrils: old vomit, cheap booze and flowery perfume, cloying, like lilies at a funeral, applied far too liberally to the necks and breasts of girls who plied their trade in sateen tops and frilly skirts. One, a redhead who had been giving him looks ever since he wandered into the place a half hour ago, had a hard face, lined around the eyes and mouth, thin lips and a certain cruelness of gaze. Or perhaps it was merely the look of a predatory animal seeking prey, in this case him and whatever greenbacks lay within his pocket. She poised herself at the bar, wearing a peek-a-boo blouse and frilly skirt, one arm draped over the edge of the counter, leaning forward just enough to offer a tantalizing glimpse of the velvety freckled flesh of her bosom.

She hadn't approached him yet, but he could tell from her manner it was only a matter of time.

He was in no mood for companionship, not tonight. He simply wanted to drink away his guilt and disappear into this nowhere little town, ride away from his profession before it rode away with him.

His gaze moved on, to another woman, standing two stools down from the redhead. She had been eyeing him, too, though perhaps more subtly. She didn't have the hard look of many bar doves. Chestnut hair fell in soft curls over her bare shoulders and a blue sateen bodice did nothing to hide the fullness of her charms. Her features carried an earthy beauty that he would have found intriguing and even desirable in another life. Cherrywood eyes reflected an intelligence and clarity that separated her from the rest of the girls of the line. But there was also something tormented in her eyes, and determined in her posture. Did she

4

recognize him, want something from him? Or was she simply a scavenger like the rest, waiting for him to get drunk enough to part with his money?

The barkeep, a man with a whiskey-veined nose who looked like a side of overly marbled beef, noticed him studying the girls, cast him an askance look. It wasn't the first time in the short while he'd been in the saloon tonight. The look told John Laramie he wasn't wanted here, in this saloon or in this town, that he best drink up and move on. Which puzzled him. Because he'd noticed the same look on a handful of other cowboys sitting at nearby tables, playing poker. It wasn't merely recognition; it was something else, something darker. But what? Fear? Yes, fear ran through this town, simmering, spreading like slow poison. But not well enough concealed to fool a man used to reading hardcases.

He reckoned he had picked the wrong damn town to try to vanish in and, truth to tell, it didn't surprise him a lick. He'd never really made the best choices since his folks passed and left him to fend for himself. He'd survived. That was about it. All the while making himself a target for the dark demons that stalked a man's soul. Why should the decision to leave his past behind be any different?

John Laramie was a hard man. Least, many a folk would have said that. The dime novel writers had built him up to be something special, a man who saved the West from the likes of vicious killers and wanton outlaws, but, hell, what made him all that different from those he tracked down and killed? If there was a solid dividing line, he damn well couldn't see it any longer. Fact was, that line was getting murkier by the day. If he didn't do something soon it would disappear completely.

You can't escape it, Laramie. You know it. The darkness rides with you. It bleeds from your soul. A man can't change who he is — what he is.

The hell he couldn't. He had to.

With a prolonged sigh he ran a hand through his dark brown hair, which came just past the tops of his ears, and his gray eyes narrowed, watery with regret. He reckoned it was no real surprise someone had recognized him, even in a town this small. Dressed in a blue bib-shirt and carrying an ivory-handled Peacemaker at his hip he looked the part of a man who tracked killers. The profession had set deep lines about his mouth and permanent dark half-moons beneath his eyes. Strands of white were just starting to touch his temples, and along with the weathered scrub of his skin from too many days under hard sunlight, it made him look a good decade older than his thirty-six years.

A small laugh, starved of humor, escaped his chapped lips. Being a hero, even on cheap paper, took its toll on a man, didn't it?

He took another swig of his whiskey and let it trickle down his throat. It occurred to him he was getting all too practiced at feeling sorry for himself. Hell, if not this town, then maybe the next would offer refuge. Maybe no one would recognize him there. He hadn't expected it to be easy. Although unwanted, his reputation dogged him, and some hothead was always willing to test it. Green outlaws looking to take a step up, or seasoned owlhoots looking to get even. His face was too well known, the likeness having appeared in far too many newspapers across the territory.

But that reputation and recognition also came with one benefit: he commanded a high price for the men he tracked down. Ranchers paid through the nose to hire him to bring down rustlers, and wealthy townsfolk or councils who needed his services rewarded him handsomely. He'd saved enough money to buy a small spread, work the land and never look back to manhunting. The area was littered with small towns and abandoned silver mines. One was like another, and tomorrow he'd move on. The devil with Lancerville and its unwelcoming folk.

Oh, hell . . .

At the bar the redhead had decided to make her move. He caught motion from the corner of his eye as she straightened and tugged her peek-a-boo blouse a bit lower. Freckles peppered her bosom, as well as her cheeks and nose. He didn't care for freckles.

But she made it no farther than a couple of paces before it seemed that the other dove with the chestnut hair and blue bodice had decided on an approach at the same instant. A whiskey bottle in her hand and a get-the-hell-out-of-my-way glint in her eyes, she shoved in front of the redhead, cutting her off, a small laugh mocking the other girl. She sashayed towards his table, cherrywood eyes locked on him, the determination in her demeanor he'd seen earlier increasing.

Six in one, half a dozen in the other, he reckoned. He didn't want company on any account.

'What the hell you think you're doin'?' the redhead said, venom in her voice, catching up and grabbing the other woman's arm. Muscles quivered in the forearm of her free hand as she balled it into a fist. She looked fully capable of taking a swing at the other dove, and he reckoned that might actually uplift his mood, and keep them both off his back for the night.

The chestnut-haired woman spun, jerked her arm free. Her lips drew tight, and her eyes narrowed. 'Stay out of my way, you boy-faced whore.' She said it in a tone so severe he almost laughed.

The redhead paused, none of the fight going out of her. 'Well, if that ain't just the pot callin' the kettle. Who the hell do you think you are? Too good for the rest of us? Why're you workin' here anyway? You don't belong.'

'I saw him first. He's mine.'

The redhead let out a scoffing *pfft*. 'Hell, you wouldn't know what to do with him.'

'I'll figure it out. I got more to work

with than you do, anyhow.' With a disdainful sneer on her full lips, the chestnut-haired woman's gaze raked the other girl's body.

The redhead glared, cheeks flooding with crimson, and an annoyed look crossed the barkeep's face. He appeared on the verge of intervening, but hesitated, perhaps worried it would cause more of a scene than was already in progress.

'Yeah,' Laramie muttered, sighing, 'you picked a hell of a town to try disappearing in.'

Another moment passed, then an icy smile slid across the redhead's lips and she backed off, returning to the bar. Something burned in that look that John Laramie didn't care for a bit — a promise to get even at some later date. But it wasn't his problem. Fact, folks' troubles were their own from now on, as far as he was concerned.

'Leave me the hell alone,' he said when the chestnut-haired woman reached him, giving him a coy turn of lip she couldn't quite pull off.

'Is that any way to treat a lady lookin' for a little friendship, gent?' She eyed his glass, then pulled the cap from her whiskey bottle and poured him two fingers.

'I didn't ask for that,' he said, irritation crawling through his veins.

'It's on the house,' she said. 'And you're welcome.' She added a smile that might have actually gotten his attention on some other night, when he wasn't feeling so damned sorry for himself. 'My name's Bethany.'

'I don't recollect asking.' He tried to sound surly and reckoned he accomplished it, but it was hard to tell, for all the effect it had on her.

'Free with the whiskey.' She pulled out a chair and seated herself, placed the bottle on the table next to his battered Stetson.

Damn, why couldn't she take the hint and just go away? 'Don't recollect askin' you to sit, neither.'

'Don't really need your permission,

gent.' Her voice held an edge that got his attention. He had run into his share of pushy whores but this woman was different, somehow.

'Go away.' His eyes narrowed.

'No.' She folded her arms beneath her breasts in defiance.

Well. That was unexpected.

His brow crinkled. 'What the hell you mean, no?'

'Opposite of yes, I reckon.'

'Judas Priest, I'm aware of what the word means. That ain't what I was askin'. I ain't interested in spending time with you and ain't paying you for such, so you're wastin' your time and mine. Git.'

'No.' Her arms tightened about herself, pushing up her bosom. He struggled to keep his gaze up where it belonged.

'Sorry?'

'I said, no. You hard of hearing?'

He peered at her, brow furrowing more deeply. Just what the hell was wrong with this woman? He'd never encountered the likes from a bargirl. He'd run into pushy ones, but normally they just got pissed off when you rejected them and stormed away looking for better prospects. Frankly he preferred it that way.

'I said I ain't payin' you for anything.'

She grinned. It was just short of maddening. 'I ain't asking you to and I ain't pleasuring you in no form, gent.'

He took a gulp of the whiskey. It suddenly tasted bitter and did nothing to help his deteriorating mood.

'All right, ma'am — '

'Bethany.'

'*Ma'am*, I ain't in the least bit of mood for this tonight. I just want to be left to my ownself.'

She leaned in, peered at him, as if studying every line on his old-before-its-years face, every stray lock of hair and every reflected bit of pain emanating from his haunted gray eyes.

'I'm not a bargirl . . . ' Her voice came low, almost a whisper. 'Least, not normally.'

He scoffed. 'So you just playing dress up . . . or down, as the case might be?'

'No.'

'You got a fondness for that word, don't you?'

'Recent one. Should have learned it sooner.' The sadness that bled into her tone took him aback. He ran a finger over his upper lip, gazed at her a long moment.

'If you ain't a bargal, what are you? And what do you want with me?'

Her voice remained low. 'You're John Laramie.'

'I'm aware of that. Been for some time. I s'pose it ain't a big surprise you recognize me. I reckon some of the others in here do, too.'

Bethany cast a sharp look about the barroom and his own gaze followed suit. The redhead was glaring at them with anger but also suspicion, as was the barkeep and a couple of other cowboys not far enough into their cups to ignore the proceedings.

'They do,' she said. 'And that isn't a

good thing. Not in this town.'

'I'd ask what the hell you meant by that but I don't give a damn.'

'You should.'

He took another drink of his whiskey. Damn, it was tasting worse by the minute.

'Hell I should. I came here to be alone. If you know who I am, then you know why I want to be left to myself.'

'I think I've established I know who you are and I knew you the moment you walked in tonight, which saved me the trouble of finding you, or someone like you.'

'Someone like me?'

'A manhunter. Bounty hunter. Professional killer . . . whatever you prefer to be called. I want to hire you.'

He almost laughed, but a sudden swooping in his head chased the notion away. Hell, he hadn't drunk that much whiskey yet; he shouldn't have been getting a case of the spins. Fact was, he could hold his liquor as well as, if not better than, any man. Nausea simmered in his belly, too.

'I ain't for hire. Fact is, miss, I'm retired.'

'You can't retire,' Bethany said, shaking her head, voice serious, still hushed.

'You really don't listen, do you?'

'Not to things I don't want to hear.'

'You best listen to me. I'm retired. I don't want no part of whatever it is you got in mind. Your husband done you wrong, find a lawyer, not a hired gun. It'll save you a bellyful of trouble.'

'Ain't married, Mr Laramie. Doubt I could tolerate a man long enough to get hitched at this moment, but that's beside the point. I need your help. Planned to do it myself, but the chance of you being successful is a lot higher.'

His hand tightened on the glass. He noticed it had started trembling a bit. 'I told you I don't want no part of whatever goods you're sellin'.'

She unwrapped her arms, leaned forward, setting her forearms on the table. 'I heard you, but I don't accept it.'

Damn. She was serious. It was in her tone and in her eyes. She was good at saying 'no' but wasn't about to take it for an answer.

'You got no choice but to accept it.'

A peculiar fuzziness had moved into the corners of his mind. Her face blurred and focused before his vision, and he shook his head. Sounds of laughter, glasses clinking and cussing in the saloon suddenly became muffled, as if somebody had jammed cotton into his ears.

'Don't I?' Were his words slurred? He felt certain they had been. Whatever the hell was wrong with him, he needed to go back to his hotel room and sleep it off. He had had enough of this woman.

He grabbed his hat and started to stand — and sat right back down in his chair. What the hell was the matter with him? His head did a doe-si-doe and his belly threatened to fly out of the saddle.

'I reckon you don't, Mr Laramie.'

She chuckled, low, without humor.

He tried to stand again, felt her arm suddenly shoved beneath his, lifting, getting him to his feet. The muscles in his legs quivered, barely able to support his weight, and sweat sprang from his forehead. It was suddenly too damn hot in the room and faces stared jumping up and down before his vision.

'What the hell — ?'

'I drugged you, Mr Laramie,' she whispered into his ear. 'I could tell the moment you came in here you were a man looking to escape his past, looking to hide. I saw your answer to my question in your eyes even before you voiced it. But I need you to do something for me and I might not get a chance like this again.'

'Told . . . told you . . . ' He couldn't make his tongue work right. It felt as thick as a sausage in his mouth and his lips tingled, went numb.

'I know what you told me.' Bethany guided him towards a stairway at the back of the room, which led to an upper floor where the doves plied their trade. 'It's all right,' she added in a louder voice, as a number of men, along with the 'keep and the redheaded bargal eyed her suspiciously and made moves to come after her. 'He just drank a bit too much and I'm gonna show him the time of his life.' She gave them a lascivious wink, and continued walking him towards the stairs before anyone could object.

He had all he could do to stay on his feet. Blackness was dancing about the corners of his mind, threatening him with unconsciousness.

He felt himself being led up the stairs, the girl helping him, much stronger than he would have thought a gal could be. He was half-conscious of her guiding him down a hall steeped in shadow and the buttery light from a low-turned wall lantern. For an instant, he gasped, as the faces of the men he had killed swirled before his mind, bathed in blood, sweating hate.

Then their haunted pleas for mercy

that never came, and the screams of the dying, filled his brain.

'No . . . ' he muttered, stumbling, only remaining on his feet by virtue of the woman holding him up.

'Yes, this time, Mr Laramie,' Bethany said, as they reached the third door down. 'You're gonna help me . . . even if it kills you.'

He struggled to form a reply, but it drowned somewhere in the blackness that overtook his consciousness.

2

The first thing John Laramie became conscious of was the thunder inside his skull. It began as a distant echo of pain, quickly rising in sharpness and intensity until it boomed in fierce waves that threatened to split his head open. Through shimmering blackness he glimpsed a vague yellowish light that pulsated in and out with his pain. The moments he lost consciousness again were a mercy, but short-lived.

The thunder increased and he was suddenly and completely awake. A groan escaped his lips and he tried to force open his eyes, closing them a heartbeat later as wan light made them sting as if icepicks had been jammed into the sockets.

He lay there a few moments — he was lying on some sort of bed, he judged, for some reason unable to move his arms or legs — praying the thunder would stop. His breath came in ragged gasps. He struggled to focus on what had happened to him, finding the memory elusive at first, then coming back in a flood of images and sounds.

He had been in the saloon, desiring nothing other than to be left to himself. A woman . . . she had asked him for help . . . then — drugged. She'd drugged him and he'd lost consciousness.

But after that . . . ?

He forced his eyes to open and the thunder in his skull doubled its roar. Nausea flooded his belly, clawed its way into his throat. It was all he could do to keep his stomach down.

'Just try to breathe easy for a short spell,' a voice came from somewhere. He could not lift his head to search for it; it lay like a leaden cannon ball on a pillow. Any effort to move it brought waves of hammering pain to his brains and sent bile searing into his throat.

'W-what . . . ?' His mouth still wasn't working right, though his tongue no longer felt thick.

'It'll clear up in a few minutes,' the voice came again. A woman, he realized this time. A woman's voice, the same woman who had drugged him. 'It's not particularly long lasting but it comes with a few unpleasant side effects.'

'Do tell . . . ' he managed to mumble, then drew a shuddering breath, and forced his stomach down. The first breath hurt like hell, made his head sing with pain, but the second came easier, the third easier still. A few moments later the thunder in his skull receded into a low throbbing drumbeat and his belly settled.

With a glance sideways, he saw the light came from a low-turned lantern sitting on a bedside table. The rest of the room was bathed in shadow, and his range of sight was limited.

He tried to move, found his arms and legs would not respond. For a moment he thought the drug had somehow paralyzed him, rendered his limbs useless. But that wasn't it. He was tied at both wrists and both ankles to either side of the brass bedposts.

He was also quite naked — except for his hat, with which the woman had kindly covered his southern parts.

'Aw, hell . . . ' he muttered, letting his head fall back to the pillow. How many times had his manhunter's sixth sense warned him of trouble on the trail, saved his life? Too many to count. He had been good at his job, damn good. He didn't make mistakes. That's what had kept him alive with every young gun and vengeance-minded hardcase looking to punch his ticket.

But it had failed him miserably this time. The woman had caught him pants down, and it was going to end here. He'd fallen for an old trick, never even suspected what she had been up to. But, then, why should he have suspected? He had retired, hadn't he? She was just a saloon gal looking to earn a dollar for a good time, same with every cowboy. But he knew he had been recognized, even in this one-horse town. He had seen it in any of a half-dozen sets of eyes. He should have been more careful. Drowning in guilt and struggling to keep the darkness away, he had made a mistake, one that was about to prove fatal, he reckoned.

The sound of a match striking brought him from his thoughts and he lifted his head. This time no spike of pain accompanied the action. The woman was right, the drug wore off nearly as fast as it came on.

A kerosene lantern flared to life and she turned the flame low, shook out the match and placed it next to the lamp on the small table. He glimpsed her features before she leaned back into a hard-backed chair, face retreating into shadow.

'Bethany . . . ' he whispered. 'Fancy meeting you here.'

'I do like a captive audience,' she said, a lifeless chuckle in her voice.

'Who'd I kill? Your husband, outlaw boyfriend, bastard kin?'

'None of the above . . . yet.'

'This ain't about revenge? Getting even for some wrong I done you?' He couldn't have told why he felt relieved by that revelation, but he did. There were times a plenty, when the darkness began to take him, he longed for death to find him, prayed an outlaw's bullet would end his life. But, suddenly confronted with the prospect, he now found that desire a lot less attractive.

'No, this isn't about vengeance, Mr Laramie . . . ' she said, her voice hardening. 'Least, not on you.'

'Then why am I here?'

'You're here because I wanted to talk you into doing me a favor, like I told you down in the saloon.'

'Might unconventional way to go about it, isn't it?'

'You were uncooperative earlier.'

'And you thought drugging me and tying me to a bed would make me

27

inclined to change my mind?'

'Like I said, captive audience. You have to listen to me now.'

'Why the hell am I naked?'

A soft chuckle came from the shadows. 'Like to say that was just for my benefit, but I figured it would slow you down should you get loose and give me time.'

'Give you time for what?'

'Why, to knock you out and tie you back up again, Mr Laramie.'

'And you planned on doin' that until — '

'Until I convinced you 'no' was the wrong answer.'

He licked his lips, sighed. ' 'No' seems to work well enough for you.'

'I'm a woman. Entitled to it. You're a manhunter, you ain't.'

'Thanks for goin' back for my hat,' he mumbled, settling his head back on the pillow.

'Least I could do. Admit I didn't have much inclination to stare at your man parts till you came around, neither.'

'Looks like I picked the wrong damn town to try to find peace in.'

'You gotta make your own peace, Mr Laramie. Running from what you are don't keep the demons away. Take it from somebody who tried to hide from her own for too many years.'

'Who says I'm running from anything?'

'Can see it in your eyes, Mr Laramie. You got the Devil chasing you and you think the trick is to run from him, hide. But it ain't that way. You have to turn around and spit in his eye.'

'You the expert on that?' A surge of irritation sizzled through his veins. For the instant he nearly forgot he was tied naked to a bed, holding a conversation with a woman who was plainly as loco as they came. He was irritated because he had to grant she might be right. For a woman he'd met — hell, he didn't even know how long he'd been unconscious — a short spell ago, she knew entirely too much about the man named John Laramie, saw too deeply into his soul. Another burst of irritation came with the notion he had to allow her a certain amount of respect for that. No other outlaw, if she was indeed an outlaw or woman of one, had ever done such.

'I ain't an expert on much, Mr Laramie,' she said after a long hesitation, her voice somber now, laced with what he took to be pain. 'But I know demons. I know running from them and trying to ignore them, pretending they don't exist while somehow you put to the back of your mind all the folks who got dead 'cause you shut your mouth and never said a word about the things you suspected or even knew absolutely. Because you lived in fear every day of your life, should you slip and say the wrong thing.'

'Reckon I got no idea what you're talkin' about, Miss — whoever the hell you are. Don't even know if Bethany's your real name.'

'Lewis. Bethany Lewis. That's my real name.'

'Ain't got a notion to say pleased to meet you, given my present position and lack of dignity.'

Another soft chuckle. 'I got me the notion you know exactly what I'm talkin' about, if in a different way. You're a brave one, Mr Laramie. Spend your life chasing down the type of man I lived in fear of. You didn't turn your back to folks in need. You didn't let others get dead because you were so scared it was easier to keep your tail between your legs than to let it trail behind you. But when it comes to who you are, *what* you are, you ain't so brave, then, are you? Your tail's right between your legs and your head's in the sand.'

The irritation running through his veins increased, though his instinct was to deny she was anywhere close to right. 'Miss Lewis — '

'You might as well call me Beth, since we're so familiar an' all.' Was that a laugh in her voice? He thought so, but didn't quite see the humor in it. He recollected never in his years chasing down men had he ever found himself in such an undignified position, and God knew he'd been in a few less than enviable entanglements when it came to bargals.

'Haven't you heard? Familiarity breeds contempt and I got a passelful of it for you right now.'

'Don't care if you hate me, long as you do what I ask.'

'No.' He reckoned he'd give her a dose of her own medicine, then wondered why he even felt the need to do so. Despite the fact she had drugged him and taken his clothes, Bethany Lewis was a woman with enough spunk to interest him under other circumstances. Other circumstances where he wasn't so all-fired pissed at her for tying him naked to a bed.

'Won't work with me, Mr Laramie. I got all the time we need to change your mind. If you'll pardon my pointing it out, you're in no position to argue.'

He hated the notion that she was

right. 'I gotta pee,' he said for little other reason than giving himself time to formulate some sort of plan for getting out of his predicament. But no solution seemed forthcoming.

'Be my guest.' She chuckled.

'Judas Priest . . . ' he muttered with a healthy measure of venom.

Another chuckle. She leaned forward, her features emerging from shadow. She looked somehow more haggard than she had earlier in the saloon, but at the same time lovelier in the soft lighting.

Hell, what was he thinking that for? She was a she-devil, for godssakes! What kind of woman went around drugging men and tying them to beds just to have a conversation?

'You ready to listen to reason, now, Mr Laramie? I got all night if you ain't.'

He sighed, resigned to the fact he was not going anywhere until he heard her out and perhaps not for a spell after that.

'What the devil do you want from me?' He gave a cursory tug at the ropes binding his wrists to the posts, found no slack, and relaxed, not wishing to scour any skin from his person.

'I thought I made that right clear earlier, Mr Laramie. I want to hire you.'

'I think I mentioned I was retired . . . right before you took a notion to steal my dignity.'

She smiled a thin smile. 'I'm working in a saloon, dressed in a bodice with my parts pouring out, Mr Laramie. Don't talk to me about dignity. We do what we have to do to make it day to day. For the first time in a long spell I'm takin' measures to set my own path and save folks, hoping in some small way to make up for those I didn't save in the past. Reckon the Almighty will be a mite more concerned with that than whether my dignity was intact.'

'You're talkin' in circles, miss. And I ain't in the mood for it.'

'It'll make sense if you stop being so bull-headed.'

The notion of her calling him

bull-headed struck him as oddly funny. 'Reckon I got nothing on you in that respect.'

'Then you'll help me?'

'No. Like I said, I'm retired.'

A heavy sigh came from the woman and for the first time he could tell he was frustrating her. That gave him a small measure of satisfaction.

'Been my observance men like you don't retire, Mr Laramie. They surrender their profession violently and permanently. Why stop doin' what you're best at?'

He shook his head on the pillow. 'I'm getting older, slower, while outlaws are getting younger and faster, more reckless, bold. Just the fact I'm tied to this bed should give you the notion I'm not at the top of my game.'

'So you're a coward?'

'I'm a realist.'

Another heavy sigh from her. Good. It was a small victory but right now he was petty enough to enjoy it.

'You're makin' excuses for somethin';

you aren't giving it up because you're old.'

'Don't rightly see how it's any of your business.'

'Oh, but it is, because I need you to take one more case.'

'And I distinctly recall telling you to go to hell.' Frustration wiped away his momentary sense of victory. He gave a yank on the ropes, instantly regretting it as the fibers cut into his wrists.

'Hell is where I am now, Mr Laramie. That should be obvious at this point.' She stood, wrapping her arms about herself and shivering visibly. For an instant her lips quivered and her cherrywood eyes went glassy with restrained tears. Then she recovered, her chin coming up in defiance of some inner demon. Her face set in hard lines and her eyes narrowed.

He blew out a heavy breath. 'What the hell you askin' me to do?' His voice came with resignation and not a little amount of exasperation.

Bethany Lewis peered at him, a thin smile appearing on her lips. She thought she had won, worn him down. And maybe she was right.

'I want you to find my brother and kill him or bring him back so I can do it.'

3

'Hell, you're more loco than I thought!' John Laramie shook his head on the pillow, which was a mistake because it still hurt to a degree.

'I'm not loco, Mr Laramie,' Bethany said. 'I'm determined to stop what's been happening. I was a coward for years, but I won't be no longer.' Her skirt rustled as she moved to the window and peered out into the night. She went silent and for the first time he was conscious of the sounds of a tinkler piano and bawdy laughter coming distantly from the saloon below. Other senses came back, now. The scents of old perfume and urine from the mattress assailed his nostrils, and soreness pained his wrists and ankles where the rope had bit into his flesh.

'Hell, you made these ropes tight enough, didn't you?' he said for no reason other than the fact that her silence bothered him more than her spouting crazy notions of wanting him to kill her brother.

'Didn't want you escaping too easy,' she said, wrapping her arms about herself again, as if to give herself courage.

'No chance of that, Calamity Beth . . .' he muttered.

She turned from the window, the lantern light falling across her face, highlighting the fear and pain now in her eyes.

'I want you to find my brother and kill him, Mr Laramie. Does that shock you?'

'A mite,' he admitted. He'd run across enough dirt in his profession that he should not have been unduly surprised this woman would ask him to do something as terrible as killing her kin, but coming from her it did, indeed, disturb him. 'He steal your petticoats and hang them from the pole or something when you were young 'uns?'

He said it half in jest, but seriousness came with his tone as well. Something dark was troubling this woman; its reflection permeated every fiber of her manner. She took stiff steps back to the chair and lowered herself on to it.

'Isn't just a case of sibling rivalry, Mr Laramie. My brother — half-brother, I should say, as my ma remarried after my pa was killed by Indians. She's dead now, too, years dead. Fact is, that no-good man of hers ran off with a saloon gal and left me and Drake — that's my brother — to fend for ourselves. I wasn't a saloon girl until a few months ago. Didn't have to be, because Drake, he took care of everything.'

She said the last with a violence that surprised him nearly as much as her request to kill her sibling.

'Then why you got a notion to have his ticket punched?'

She hesitated, looked towards the window for long moments, then back to him. 'Drake . . . he was always different.

I reckon a lot of it was because his pa beat him so much. I saw the bruises the day he came into my ma's homestead and they would appear on his arms and legs and face every so often, like they just sprung up by magic or something, because I never heard him being beaten. His pa waited till me and my ma were asleep and Drake . . . Drake he never screamed or cried. Was like he couldn't cry. His pa had knocked all the tears out of him.'

'Then how do you know he was beat?'

'Drake told me finally, right after he found me alone in the barn one day . . . ' A tear streaked down her cheek and the darkness in her tone grew deeper.

'Oh, hell . . . ' Laramie muttered, taking the notion he didn't like where this was going and suddenly seeing why a half-sister might want to hire a manhunter.

'Whatever you're thinkin', Mr Laramie, is likely right. Drake was always keeping something inside himself, some kind of fury at his pa. Got to a point where he couldn't control it no more. He needed to let it loose, to control others. I was only thirteen when he got me in the barn. I didn't cry, either. He told me if I did he would kill me. I believed him. After it was over, he told me his pa beat him. Told me some other things that sonofabitch did to him, too, which I won't trouble you with. Tellin' you this just because I want you to understand why Drake is the way he is, and it ain't easy admitting what happened.'

'And that's why you want me to kill him?'

'No . . . no, it isn't. You see, powerful loco as it sounds, Mr Laramie, I forgave him for what he did to me that day. My ma had always took me to church, made sure I knew the Lord wished us to forgive, if not forget.'

'Sounds like you got over that.'

She offered a thin smile. 'No, not entirely. I reckon that's the only way my ma was able to forgive the things her fella did, because she caught him with whores in town more times than I can recollect.' She paused, with the back of her hand brushing the stray tear from her cheek.

'Then why — '

'Comin' to that, Mr Laramie. Give me time. Never told this to anyone before and it don't come out like a greased pig.' Her gaze went back to the window and a small shiver went through her body. 'See, that wasn't the last time Drake . . . got familiar with me. Every time his pa beat him, Drake, he'd come lookin' for me. His pa controlled him, then Drake'd control me. After, he'd always come out with some awful thing his pa had done to him. Once confessed his pa had killed his ma in a fit of anger. I was worried 'bout my own ma after that — you know what it's like to fear every day of your life, Mr Laramie?'

'Got a notion . . . '

'I'm sure you do.' She gazed back at him. ' 'Cept you're afraid of what's inside you, not of other men. I was afraid for my ma, afraid of Drake and his pa. Even after his pa took off, that fear went on.'

'Drake stayed behind . . . ?'

She nodded, taking a sharp breath as if to steel herself against her memories. 'He did. He got tired of . . . well, doin' the thing he was doin' to me, instead going into town and seeing bargals. He beat up a few of them pretty bad. Recollect one time the marshal came a-callin' and was going to arrest Drake. Most folks didn't give a damn about saloon gals but Marshal Haney, he did.'

'Then why isn't he in jail?' Laramie felt a lead ball settling in his belly. Any feelings for his own predicament for the moment had been replaced by anger towards a man he did not know, Drake Lewis.

'Because Drake cut his throat, Mr Laramie. Marshal, he turned his back a second, but it wasn't his fault. Drake, he could talk a nun out of her habit. He had a way of hidin' the bad side of

44

himself from folks when he wanted to. Was like he was two different men, sometimes. But I reckon I can understand that after having to keep quiet for so many years when his pa beat him.'

'Nobody noticed the marshal was missing?'

'Oh, they noticed. Deputy came snoopin' around but Drake convinced him the marshal had ridden off. Drake had . . . ' Bethany shuddered, the horror of a past event flashing in her dark eyes. 'He took an axe to the marshal's body, fed the remains to the pigs. Took the man's horse out somewhere and shot it, too.'

'Aw, hell . . . ' Laramie muttered, belly roiling. He had run across some bad types in his day, but Drake Lewis, if what Bethany was telling him was true, was the worst of the lot.

'Gets worse, Mr Laramie. Drake just got angrier and angrier after that. He'd throw fits, strike me. Told me if I ever told a soul about what I seen I'd be joinin' the marshal. Couple of saloon gals disappeared, the first bein' the one who'd told the marshal. Drake didn't say nothin' about it, but I knew he did it. And I didn't say a word. I was too scared. I held my tongue and watched while Drake did whatever he wanted to whoever he wanted.'

'Where is he now?' Fury was coursing through Laramie's veins like poison. Hell, he hadn't wanted to get involved in this woman's plight, but everything she told him reminded him of the reasons he had become a manhunter in the first place: the duty he saw within himself to protect innocent folk from men like Drake Lewis. For a moment the dark anger inside him clawed to get free, over-whelm him. It ignited the desire to kill Drake Lewis, slowly, punish him for every moment of terror he had caused this woman.

No, he told himself. He couldn't let it take over. He had come here to leave his past, and the killing, behind.

'Comin' to that, Mr Laramie.' She

shuddered again. 'You see, Drake was always bad. I came to realize that it wasn't just what his pa had done to him. It was something in his blood, in the Lewis blood.'

'You're a Lewis,' Laramie said.

'I'm not a Lewis by birth — my ma made me take Drake's pa's last name. I was a Masterson before. Drake's evil was like a sickness his pa passed on to him. Drake would have gone bad even if his pa had treated him decent. Just a matter of time. I made excuses for his behavior for years. Reckon it was just my own fear of him and what he'd do to me.

'Drake was bad, and he got in with some bad men. He'd have them over, let them take turns with me, Mr Laramie. I ain't tellin' you that for sympathy and it's damned hard to admit. Just givin' you all the facts.'

The darkness inside John Laramie surged up again and he was barely able to hold it at bay. The thought of what this woman had experienced nearly drove him to rage.

'I'm . . . sorry . . . ' he said at last, not knowing quite what to say.

'Don't be . . . ' she whispered. 'Least, not for me. I let things go on too long because I was a coward. I don't deserve pity.' He would have begged to differ but saw no point debating it with her at the moment.

'Drake and his men . . . ' she continued. 'You heard 'bout the robberies and killings in these parts?'

He nodded. 'I heard rumors of a small gang, the Cross Gang they call themselves. Murdered a few bargals, stage drivers. Got away with a lot of cash and jewelry.'

She winced, as if the recounting actually cut her. 'Drake, he called his gang that because of my ma always going on 'bout her churchin'. His pa told her one day that the only thing that came from the cross was death, look what happened to Jesus. He thought it was funny. Drake did, too. Apple don't fall far, as they say.' She paused, licked her lips, and let out a small scoffing sound. 'I told Drake once it wasn't so funny to mock other folks' cherished beliefs. Don't know what fit of courage came over me to make me say such a thing to him. I knew better. He taught me hard not to say it again.'

'Yet here you are,' Laramie said, fighting with every ounce of his will to keep the fury from overtaking him.

She nodded, brow furrowing. 'Here I am. I watched for a couple years how he would come back nights, always with money, even necklaces he would some-times give to me after he let his men use me. Like he was askin' forgiveness or tryin' to show me if I did what he wanted I would be rewarded. Times, I wondered why he didn't just kill me. Even prayed he would because I couldn't stand the fear anymore. I just cowered, let it go on. Till one day Drake up and left with his gang. He was just gone. Left a note telling me I was free. I don't know why. Made no sense, as I saw it. Left a bunch of money and some jewelry on a table in the parlor, too. I was scared again, but for a whole different reason. For years I hadn't known anything else but fear and keepin' my mouth shut. On the day he left I realized I was afraid because what was going to happen would take courage, courage I never felt before.'

'How long ago was this?' Laramie asked.

'Six months past.'

'Why you workin' in a saloon, if he left you that money?'

'Part of my penance, Mr Laramie. That money and those jewels Drake left, they had blood on them and after a week on my own I had a revelation just how much of a fool and coward I had been. I couldn't always see it when he was around, makin' me fear. Once he was gone, everything my ma had taught me before she married that sonofabitch came floodin' back. I was just as guilty as him for those folks he got dead, because I didn't tell anyone, didn't try to stop him.'

'You were a woman alone, afraid. He would have killed you had you tried to tell anyone, way he did that marshal.'

She offered a weak smile. 'Be that as it may, Mr Laramie, I knew I couldn't use that money unless it was to right a wrong. I used some to survive, found a way to live by using the only thing I had, my body, while I searched for my brother. Took me a spell to track him here.'

Shock flashed on John Laramie's face. 'He's here, in Lancerville?'

'Somewhere abouts. This town . . . you see the fear in their eyes when you came in?'

'I noticed something, wasn't sure what.'

'It's him, I know it. I lived with that fear too many years not to recognize it. I tried town after town. I know my brother's patterns, Mr Laramie. Despite his hate and meanness, he's got one flaw I could use against him; he's a creature of habit and grounded to his roots. He wouldn't go far from his foundation two towns over.'

'So you tried the surrounding towns until you found one living in fear?'

She nodded. 'Been here a week; got me a job in the saloon. They didn't really want to hire me and that redheaded gal, Lily, she's the only one not lookin' afeared, least not in the same way the 'keep and some of the other folks are.'

'Marshal?'

'Reckon he's as scared as the rest. Ain't much of a lawman, but I reckon this town never really needed much law till my brother started comin' in.'

'*Why* is he comin' in?'

'Women, food, maybe he has someone helping him fence the jewels. I reckon they're holed up around these parts somewhere close.'

'What if he sees you?'

'I want him to. Then I can kill him myself.' Her hand dipped into the valley between her breasts, came back out with a derringer. 'I won't be afeared of him anymore, Mr Laramie. And I won't let him kill more innocent folk.'

'How'd you know I'd be here? I told no one.'

She replaced the small gun into her bodice. 'I didn't. But I recognized you. My brother kept tabs on the major manhunters in the area. One of his men reads their dime novels, even. But the moment I saw you I knew if anyone could find him and stop him from killing folks it was you . . . 'cept I saw something in your eyes, too. I knew you didn't want to be found. Studied you a spell before comin' over to your table. Noticed the redhead lookin' your way, too.'

'So you figured I wouldn't be interested in helping out and decided to drug me?'

'I suspected you might want to be left alone. I couldn't take the chance you wouldn't help me. If it hadn't been you, I would have got some other man-hunter eventually, if I wasn't able to find my brother and kill him myself.'

'Where'd you get the drug? Just

happen to be carryin' it around?'

She smiled. It wasn't a pleasant smile. 'My brother left some behind. He would use it sometimes on gals who didn't want to part with their pleasures, gals who didn't work the saloon. He got himself a hankerin' for church girls sometimes. Reckon it's a peculiarity of his. I had it on me, case I needed to use it on him. When I figured you might not be co-operative . . . '

'You put it in the whiskey bottle you used to pour me a drink.'

She nodded. 'Reckon I should apologize for that . . . and your position.'

'Looks like you picked up some bad habits from him,' he said with not a little accusation in his tone.

Her head dropped and she stared at the floor for a long moment, then looked back up. 'I'm not perfect, Mr Laramie. And I've learned to take advantage when I have to. Was wrong doin' what I done to you. I know that and I'm truly sorry. But he's evil, Drake is. And he has to be stopped.'

'And the end justifies the means?'

She nodded again. 'I'm sorry, but yes, long as nobody gets killed. I want your help and I read you're a man of your word, so if you say you will help I will believe you. At any rate, you know what I want, now. No point in keepin' you prisoner anymore.'

She stood, reached to the table and picked up an object that had remained in the shadows. The blade of a Bowie knife glinted with reflected lantern light in her hand. As she approached the end of the bed, he got the awful feeling she was going to go to work on him with the knife and his heart skipped a beat.

She sliced through the ropes holding his ankles. 'I ain't the type to beg, Mr Laramie, but please . . . please help me stop him from killing anyone else. I am well aware it won't redeem my past, but it's the only way I even know how to attempt to go into my future.'

She moved to the head of the bed, sliced the ropes holding a wrist, then went to the other side and repeated the action. She backed away, tossing the knife to the bureau top.

'Clothes are on the chair . . . ' She ducked her chin to another hardbacked chair on the opposite side of the nightstand.

Laramie sat up, his head spinning and the nausea returning. He was careful to keep the hat about his middle, modesty suddenly a priority to him again. He fought to recover from the drug effects, suppressing the sickness after a moment and stopping his vision from jittering.

'You gonna turn around?' he asked.

'Why should I?' she said with a small laugh. 'Already seen everything you got to offer and I stopped worrying about being a lady a long time ago.'

After an awkward moment and a flush of heat reddening his face he managed to pull on his clothes, strap his gunbelt to his waist, and return the hat to his head, where it belonged.

'Will you help me, Mr Laramie?'

Bethany asked after he had dressed.

'Could take you in for kidnapping and probably a host of other things,' he said, annoyance lacing his tone.

'You could.' She stepped close, placed her palms on his chest. He couldn't deny liking the feeling.

Dammit, he thought. He had come here looking for peace, a chance to hold off the darkness threatening to overcome him. But if what this gal had told him was true, Drake Lewis belonged at the end of a rope. If he didn't find this man, more innocent folks would die and he would be as responsible for inaction as Bethany had been.

He had to admit it: for one of the few times in his career he was afraid. Not of Drake Lewis or his ilk, not of possible death, but of what one more case might do to him, how it might break down the wall he was carefully building between himself and the darkness inside.

He peered at her, and for that instant she looked so ... vulnerable, so helpless. She was not the hard woman who had suffered under the control of another, she was just a woman needing help, desperately.

'All right, I'll find him,' he said at last. 'And if what you tell me is true, I'll bring him to justice.'

'No, I want him dead.' The venom was back in her voice and her face tightened.

He nodded. 'More often than not I bring them in that way, but if I don't he'll hang, you have my word.'

She seemed to deflate then, shuddering, as if everything she had used to build herself a façade of courage suddenly came down in one relieved crash. She came to her toes, pressed her lips to his before he could pull back. The kiss lingered a moment, and he reckoned he damn well liked it.

She spun, went to the door and pulled it open. 'Thank you, Mr Laramie,' she said, pausing with her hand on the handle. 'I'll give you whatever money you want afterward.'

He shook his head. 'This ain't for

money this time. You'll be here at the saloon if I find anything?'

'I'll be at the hotel, Room 14. My bargal days are done . . . ' She turned and stepped out into the hall.

Thunder came with her exit. This time, however, it came not from the inside of his skull but from the hallway beyond the door.

A shot.

'Nooo!' he yelled, rage flooding his veins. He was in motion before it stopped echoing, hand sweeping towards the Peacemaker in the holster at his hip. But it was too late.

Bethany staggered backward as if kicked by a mule, crashed into the door jamb and slid to the floor.

4

John Laramie reached the door in a heartbeat, surging rage robbing him of most caution. A glance had told him Bethany Lewis had been seriously wounded and he cursed himself for not somehow saving her.

There was nothing he could have done, and he knew it, but that didn't matter. He'd spent the better part of his life tracking down killers, wanted men, saving innocent lives, and now when it might have mattered the most he had failed.

Another shot came and a section of the doorjamb disintegrated, sending splinters spiraling through the air. One brushed his cheek, stinging, opening a small cut.

He jerked to a halt, caution suddenly taking hold, as a third shot crashed through the hallway and lead drilled into the wall near the door.

His heart thundered in his chest and beads of sweat formed on his brow. Damn, it wasn't like him to be this shaken, but a surging panic over the young woman was driving him to make foolish moves.

Time. He didn't have much. She didn't have much. Another glance at her form, propped in a sitting position against the jamb, blood soaking through her bodice above her abdomen and between her fingers as she tried to stanch the flow by pressing her trembling hand against the wound, told him she needed a sawbones if she were to have any chance of living out the next hour.

He counted: one, two, three . . . no more shots came. He pressed himself to the door, Peacemaker coming up beside his cheek, finger itching to pull the trigger. A soft moan came from Bethany and he swallowed hard.

She's just a girl, Laramie, and this is just another mission. Get hold of yourself!

He eased around the door, chanced a gaze into the hall.

The man was waiting for him, instantly triggered another shot. Lead gouged splinters from the edge of the door.

Laramie jerked back into the room; another bullet punched into the wall where his head had been a second before.

He whirled, fury making him reckless; but it was a calculated recklessness. The shooter wouldn't expect the move, would expect that the last shot had put fear into John Laramie. But Laramie feared no man. He had been seasoned in brimstone and blood, and this shooter was something solid, unlike the darkness inside him, something he could deal with. Something he could kill.

As he whirled into the hall, he did so in a half-crouch, knees bending just inches, Peacemaker swinging up and around before him.

His finger hit the trigger instantly, without much aim, merely instinct and skill, and sent lead towards where he had glimpsed the man to be only seconds before.

If he was wrong, he would die.

Ice flowed through his veins as he executed the move, a familiar, welcomed feeling, the way it did each time he moved in for the kill. The darkness, welling, taking over, detaching him from the fact that the man shooting was just that — a man, like himself, if one corrupted by circumstance and his own nature.

Kill him!

Three shots crashed through the dimly lit hallway. The low-turned flame in the wall lantern jittered, causing shadows and amber light to waver on the walls like demons dancing. Dark demons. On the walls and inside John Laramie.

He had judged right. The man was where he had been before, standing at the top of the stairs leading to the barroom proper, gun raised, hard face locked with sudden terror.

But he had misjudged, too, in his hasty aim. Lead drilled into the wall next to the man, one bullet scoring a furrow across the hardcase's shoulder, tearing through blue denim and soft flesh.

A squawk came from the shooter and he whirled, nearly losing his balance and plunging down the stairs head first. He recovered in time to bound down the steps, three at a time.

'Christ!' Laramie said with a hiss. His gaze swept back to Bethany, who hadn't moved. He jumped to her, knelt. The wound was bad, worse than he had thought. If the bullet had punctured her intestine . . .

He snatched a bandanna from his shirt pocket, jammed it beneath her bloody fingers.

'Press this to the wound. I'll fetch the doc.' He couldn't keep the worry out of his tone.

Bethany's eyelids fluttered, and dullness blunted the bright cherrywood. 'That . . . man . . . one of Drake's . . . '

A chill swept through Laramie's rugged form. 'Then he knows you're here after him . . . or thinks that I am . . . '

'G-go . . . after . . . ' Her eyelids fluttered closed and cold fingers closed around his heart.

'No . . . ' he muttered, for just a second frozen to where he knelt. 'Dammit, Bethany, hold on . . . '

He was up and sprinting towards the stairs a heartbeat later, using far less caution than his years of tracking vicious owlhoots had taught him.

Reaching the top of the stairs he paused. From below came the sounds of clipped yelps and the piano suddenly stopped. A bargirl cried out.

Laramie took the stairs in a series of bounds, every nerve burning with the desire to put a bullet between the hardcase's eyes. All thoughts of guilt or restraint vanished in the heat of rage.

He spotted the man, who had just reached the batwings, casting a glance over his shoulder, to see Laramie at the bottom of the stairs. The hardcase uttered a hoarse laugh, a mocking laugh. He obviously knew Laramie was in no position to fire at him without risking hitting one of the saloon patrons. He had no such qualms and fired off a shot that chipped wood from the banister.

'Stop him!' Laramie shouted, raising his Peacemaker towards the man, though he could not risk firing. A dark thought told him that it would be worth the collateral damage to take down a man who worked for a vicious killer and who was likely one himself.

The man, sudden panic swiping at his features as he pulled the trigger again and discovered his gun to be empty, plunged through the batwings.

The barkeep glared at him and a number of other cowboys cast him fearful glances. The red-headed bargal was leaning against the far end of the bar, peering at him with a half-spiteful, half-amused look on her features.

'What the hell is wrong with you

folks?' he yelled, making his way across the barroom towards the batwings. 'Why didn't you stop him?'

'Ain't our place to get involved, mister,' a man said, shaking his head, fear trembling in his tone. In that instant, Laramie knew that everything Bethany had told him was the truth. Drake Lewis was using this town and held the folks within it in a grip of terror. They didn't dare lift a finger to stop one of his men.

'Get the doc!' Laramie yelled back at them as he reached the batwings. 'The bargirl's been gut shot. Get him now, goddammit!'

He plunged through the batwings, heedless of the fact that the man might be lying in ambush for him and had probably reloaded on the run. What the devil was clouding his usual skill and caution? He had a notion it was worry over that young woman lying wounded upstairs. He hadn't known her more than a few hours, if he judged right, but she had gotten to him. Something about her life and hard times played on his sympathy and compassion, made him want to protect her.

Hell of a job he had done.

The night air slapped his face with a brisk chill that shook him from his recklessness. No one was out on the street, which was fortunate, given the situation.

He skirted sideways, bending low, gun clenched in his hand so tight that tendons stood out like telegraph cables.

Barely in time. The roar of a gunblast filled the street, and a flash of fire from the muzzle of a Smith & Wesson came from across the street. The bullet went wide, ploughed into the side of a shop. Two more shots followed, chasing Laramie's heels as he got behind a barrel.

Three shots.

Laramie's own gun came up, a blur of motion. His finger spasmed on the trigger and two shots came almost as one.

Across the street the hardcase scurried along the boardwalk, both the bullets missing him and drilling into walls. A short squeal came from the man's lips. A coward, like all his kind, Laramie reckoned. Fine at ambushing but a runner when someone shot back. He fired a backward panic-inspired shot that hit entirely too close to the manhunter out of pure luck.

Four . . .

Laramie scooted along the board-walk, seeking to get a bead on the hardcase, who weaved in a zigzagging pattern, obviously used to trying to save his worthless hide. He dove behind barrels, supporting beams, behind a wagon standing near the general store.

Laramie fired again, and lead gouged wood from a beam. The shooter whirled, fired a backward shot that came nowhere near Laramie, then drove onward, heading for an alley a few dozen feet ahead.

Five . . .

Laramie took a chance. The man was scared, wasn't aiming carefully and the distance made it hard enough to hit anything with the gun he was toting. The manhunter leaped from the boardwalk into the wide main street, hit the ground running, arrowing towards the shooter.

The shooter fired again, his aim worsening. Lead dug into the hard-packed dirt.

Six shots . . . Kill him now, Laramie! You know you want to. He shot Bethany. He deserves to die, the way they all do!

The darkness inside him raged up again, seeking to gain control, and in that moment he was damn near ready to let it.

Palming the hammer, he triggered a shot — but the hammer fell on an empty chamber. Hell, he had emptied his own gun. The only stroke of luck was that the other man had also emptied his, if Laramie had counted right.

As he ran his fingers pried at the bullets tucked in his belt. He'd learned early on to reload on the fly and a moment later the chambers were full again.

The gunman reached the alley. He whirled, triggered a last shot, aim perfect this time. If Laramie had misjudged he would be dead in the street. But he hadn't. A hollow clack sounded in the brittle night air. The gunman uttered a chopped yell, then hurled his empty gun at the onrushing manhunter, who sidestepped, avoiding the weapon.

Laramie fired, hoping to plug the man before he got into the alley, but the hardcase's speed was driven by renewed fear. Unarmed, a manhunter with a full load on his heels, he was suddenly the prey, no longer the hunter. He leaped from the end of the boardwalk and Laramie's bullet whined over the hardcase's head, ricocheting from the building corner.

The shooter dove into the alley, vanishing in the glut of darkness.

Laramie uttered a sharp curse under his breath, shifted towards the alley.

He needed this man, he realized, suddenly relieved that he had not hit him fatally. He had reacted from raw emotion, instead of rationality. That's what the darkness did. It killed, without question, without remorse, without prudence. Drake Lewis held this town in a grip of fear and inaction. That would make finding him and bringing him to justice much harder. Too many folks could be protecting the outlaw. The shooter was his only lead.

Laramie reached the alley, slowed. He didn't know that the hardcase might not have some concealed smaller gun or knife, and the darkness of the alley was intense compared to the hanging lantern-lit gloom of the street.

After easing to the side of a building, he pressed his back to the wall, gun ready in his hand. He peeked around the corner of the building.

'You best come on out,' he said, voice sharp and carrying. 'I can see the other end's blocked.' His gray eyes narrowed as he tried to pierce the darkness. He could barely pick out the bulky dark shapes of stacked crates and barrels littering the alley, but it was clear it was a dead end; no light bled from a parallel street. He couldn't distinguish the form of the shooter, however. The man was hiding behind a crate or barrel, waiting. That made him a cornered animal, and Laramie had to be careful. Scared men took chances, struck with desperation.

He slipped into the shadows of the alley, noticing his hand tightening to an uncomfortable degree on his Peacemaker. Perhaps what he had told Bethany about getting too old for this job was true. While he was still fast enough on the draw, emotions and doubts were starting to get in the way. That would get him killed sooner rather than later — unless he let that darkness take over, guide him.

No! I can't let it win.

Images pried at his mind, the pleading bloody faces from his nightmares. He forced them away, the hairs on the back of his neck suddenly prickling, warning him that —

Something leaped out from behind a barrel, a lunging blot of deeper blackness that became a man.

Laramie tried to swing his gun around but his lapse in focus cost him. The man hit him full force before he could aim.

The impact sent Laramie stumbling backward. The gun went off in his hand, a flash of flame from its muzzle illuminating his attacker a second before the Peacemaker, jolted by the recoil of the unexpected shot, flew from his grip. The bullet drilled into the opposite wall, missing the shooter.

Laramie slammed into the wall, rebounded; the hardcase was ready for him. He snapped a fist into Laramie's face as the manhunter came forward, doubling the force.

Stars exploded before Laramie's eyes and his legs threatened to buckle. A harsh laugh crashed into his ears.

'You ain't so tough after all, Hell on Hoofs, are ya?' The man's voice was harsh but despite the bravado it held a healthy measure of fear. This man was frightened and had sought to cover it with a boast, giving Laramie the instant he needed to recover.

Vision still partly blurred, he pistoned a fist into the man's abdomen.

The sound of a chopped squawk and the harsh expulsion of air came from the hardcase's lips. He doubled, and Laramie tried to deliver an uppercut, put him down.

The hardcase, whether from instinct or fear, straightened like a loosed stage-spring and swung a right cross that sent pain cascading through Laramie's teeth and rattled his skull. His legs threatened to go two different directions. He wasn't sure what held him up. The man was strong, desperate, and the blow connected flush. Another hit like that and the hardcase would finish him.

With a shake of his head and a guttural sound, Laramie surged forward, adrenaline overriding the haze before his eyes and quivering in his legs.

He swung, with little sense of skill or planning, just blind rage, forcing the hardcase to back off and allow Laramie time to regain his senses completely.

The hardcase stumbled backwards across the alley towards a stack of crates. Laramie's sudden ferocity had taken him by surprise, stunned him.

The manhunter cocked an arm and the hardcase let out a panicked yell. In a desperate move, he grabbed the crate beside him and yanked. Crates came tumbling down, right as Laramie's fist lashed out.

They hit him hard and an instant later he was on the ground beneath them, unhurt but momentarily pinned.

He uttered a sharp curse and flung the crates off, but the hardcase's running bootsteps were already retreating into the distance.

By the time Laramie had reached his feet, located his gun and staggered from the alley, the shooter was long gone.

'Dammit,' Laramie muttered, holstering his gun. He couldn't have bungled that any worse had he tried. He was lucky he hadn't gotten himself killed.

He swept those thoughts aside as the image of Bethany lying at the foot of the door came crashing back into his mind. He swiped a dribble of blood from his forehead where one of the crates had hit, hastened back to the saloon.

The barkeep and a number of the cowboys stared at him as he shoved through the batwings. He couldn't tell whether it was with fear, hate or expectancy. Did they want the hardcase dead, or him?

'Where's the doc?' he said, voice jabbing through the silence.

No one answered. The redheaded bargal let out a small chuckle, and the barkeep, standing before the counter, looked away.

'Where is he?' Laramie shouted, fury tightening his face.

'No one got him,' the 'keep answered, swallowing hard, his gaze refusing to meet Laramie's.

Laramie was suddenly next to the man, grabbing two handfuls of his shirt and forcing his face close. 'What the goddamn hell you mean, no one got him?'

'We can't get involved, mister,' the redhead answered, her tone all too casual.

'S-she's right,' the barman stammered. 'You don't know what he'll do . . . '

'You don't know what I'll do,' Laramie said, suppressing a dark urge to break the man's neck. 'Where's he located — tell me!' Laramie's voice had become a crashing shout. More than one of the cowboys jolted at the sound of it.

'At — at the edge of town, south. You can't miss it.' The 'keep's voice shook and his eyelids fluttered.

Laramie pressed his face closer. 'That girl upstairs dies and I'll be back to take it out on you, understand me?'

The barkeep nodded a rabbitlike nod and Laramie shoved him back against the bar.

'You best have a buckboard ready for me outside by the time I get back down here. Ain't no telling what I'll do if you don't.' He whirled, stalked across the saloon; men parted to let him pass. They were afraid of Drake Lewis, he was positive, but in that moment they were more afraid of him.

He went back to the room upstairs. Bethany hadn't moved but he noted a distressing amount of blood soaking her bodice and the bandanna pressed to the wound.

He went to her, knelt. She had lost consciousness and her skin was a grayish color he damn well didn't like. He forced down the surge of worry that rose in his gut and gently slid one hand behind her back and the other beneath her knees. He lifted, coming to his feet with her in his arms.

'Don't die on me, woman,' he muttered, voice wavering. He carried her down the hallway, then the stairs. No one got in his way as he headed to the batwings.

Someone had taken his threat seriously, because a buckboard waited outside. He lay her as gently as possible in the back, then climbed into the driver's seat.

It took only a few moments to locate the sawbones's place, but he had lost far too much time already. He had underestimated the fear Drake Lewis had put into the townsfolk. He hadn't thought they would let the woman suffer, die. He had been wrong.

'Goddamn town,' he said under his breath as he reined to a halt and hopped from the seat. The whole bunch deserved whatever Drake Lewis gave them. Maybe he'd let them save their own sorry asses.

He went to the door of the small homestead, pounded a fist against the wood. The place was dark, the sawbones likely gone to bed. A small carved sign on the door said: Dr Stanley Briscoe.

'Hold your damn horses!' a voice, laced with sleep and gruffness, yelled from within. A light came on inside the house, its buttery glow washing through the front window. A bolt lock clacked on the other side and the door swung open. A man in a nightshirt stood before him, gray hair a-tussle, old eyes clouded with sleep.

'What the devil you want this late?' the doc said, then peered closer at Laramie, and lost any defiance he might have been considering. 'Hell, what's wrong?'

Laramie went back to the buckboard, gently lifted Bethany from the back and carried her to the door.

The doctor's features went grim and he motioned the manhunter inside. They went through a small front waiting room with hard-backed chairs and a desk to another that held a number of cabinets stocked with bottles of tablets and liquids. An examination table stood in the center of the room and Laramie carried the girl to it, set her down.

'Wait out there,' the doc said,

nodding his head towards the door. Laramie nodded, reluctant, but backed to the door and went to the waiting room.

The doc closed the door behind him and the sudden silence rattled the manhunter's nerves more than chasing the hardcase had. He had never been a patient man, but this was worse. Something about that woman in there . . . she *had* to live. She deserved to live, get her second chance, her shot at redemption. She deserved it more than a man like John Laramie did. She had not chosen her lot; he had chosen his, and death stalked him every day.

God help Drake Lewis if she didn't make it.

*   *   *

'Where the hell have you been?' asked the man wearing a duster. He was standing by the window, his back to two other men in the small cabin. His head lifted as the door swung closed but he did not turn. His reflection in the glass appeared to be made of stone. Lantern light glimmered upon black pomaded hair, slicked back tight enough to reveal a pronounced widow's peak. His broad shoulders were pulled back, anger causing a distinct rigidness to his carriage.

The man who had entered stopped, panic flashing across his hard face. 'I-I had me some trouble in town when I went after that manhunter.'

The man at the window turned, annoyance causing shivers of fire to sear through his being. His hard green eyes pinned the man, narrowed. 'I don't like trouble, Simpson. Reckon you know that by now. When I give one of my men a job, I expect it done right. Got me a notion that ain't what happened.'

The hardcase nodded, a rabbitlike movement, took a step forward, licked his lips. The other two men, their weathered faces betraying worry as well, didn't move, merely stared at the man who'd entered, as if expecting lightning to strike him dead right where he stood.

That satisfied Drake Lewis. Indeed, it did.

The cabin was tiny, only four bedrolls on the floor, a small card-table, upon which lay scattered remnants of a poker game, and another small table holding a blue enameled coffee pot being the only furniture in the room. Drake Lewis didn't need much when he was hiding out and what he did need he went into town and took.

'He's dead?' Drake's voice came somber, dirge-like. 'Tell me he's dead, Simpson. I'd be downright displeased if that weren't the case.'

The hardcase named Simpson shuddered visibly, appeared on the verge of bolting for the door. 'He . . . he's better than we thought. I missed him.'

A shadow passed over Drake's face. He couldn't abide failure, not one damned bit. 'You knew his rep. They call him Hell on Hoofs for a reason.

84

Expected you to make adjustments for that fact.'

The man shook again and a wet stain appeared at the crotch of his britches. His eyes darted and sweat trickled from his brow.

'Drake, we weren't expectin' him to come into town lookin' for you.' Simpson's voice came with a plea for mercy.

A thin laugh escaped Drake Lewis's lips. His hand went to his nose, finger sliding back and forth over the slight crook for a moment.

'You knew he'd be there tonight. You knew my sister was trying to hire him. But there's more, isn't there, Simpson? I can see it in your eyes. You didn't kill him and you didn't get caught . . . so that means something else has you shaking like a goddamn newborn calf.'

Simpson's dull eyes watered; a tear slipped from one of them to streak down his face. 'Please, Drake . . . it was an accident, I swear it was!'

'What happened?' No compromise

came in Drake Lewis's tone. Just ice and condemnation. An utter lack of mercy or compassion. He didn't like the way Simpson was behaving and cold fingers tightened in his belly. He noticed the man's gun was missing from its holster, as well.

'Your sister . . . ' Simpson appeared on the verge of collapse. Drake motioned with his head to the other two men, Cleves and Jones, and they each grabbed one of Simpson's arms, holding him up.

'What about my sister, Simpson?' Drake's tone became even colder and his eyes became green ice. The annoyance in his veins swelled into barely restrained rage.

'She — she came out of the room . . . I-I thought it was Laramie . . . '

Drake took a step closer to the man. His arm whipped up, the back of his fist crashing into the man's jaw. Simpson's head rocked and he let out a small bleat of pain.

'Please, Drake, please, it wasn't my

fault. I didn't know she'd come out, I swear I didn't know!'

'What the hell happened to my sister?' Drake's voice exploded from his mouth. Simpson shook his head, mouth opening, closing, no sound coming out. 'Tell me, goddammit!'

'I shot her, Drake,' Simpson said in a sputter, blood running from his lips. 'It was an accident, oh Christ, I swear it was. She, she came out first. Thought it was, was Laramie. Please, Drake . . . '

Drake Lewis stood frozen for a moment, for one of the few times in his life so overcome with fury he couldn't move. Images from the past flashed across his mind, colored by a blood fever.

No, Pa, please don't hit me . . .

Screams and pleas, ringing through his mind, bellowing from the black corners of his memory.

A boy, six, maybe seven, on his knees, beseeching his pa as the old bastard's fist raised, then flashed down. Bone throbbing and flesh breaking. Pain, ungodly pain. And fear, freezing fear.

You never do nothin' right, do ya, boy? Yer just a no-good worthless piece of dung!

The images stopped suddenly, as he regained control. His gaze focused on Simpson; cowering, weak Simpson, who reminded him of the a-feared little boy he had been. Simpson, who had shot his sister. He'd let his sister go free, given her a chance, but she had chosen to track him for some reason. He'd watched her, watched her close, but Laramie was unexpected and it told him all he needed to know: Bethany wanted him dead. And for the first time in his life he admired the strength she had finally shown. Not that it would have saved her life had she come after him.

'Is she dead?' Drake asked, his voice lowering, deadly.

The stain at Simpson's crotch expanded. 'Please, Drake, please — '

Drake grabbed the man's face, fingers gouging into either cheek, and he forced Simpson to look into his eyes. 'I asked you, you sonofabitch. Is. She. Dead?'

'I dunno, Drake, I swear I dunno. Laramie came after me and I ran and got away.'

Drake didn't say a word for a moment, then he released the man's chin and patted the side of Simpson's face, a grim expression taking his lips.

'Please, Drake . . . I'll get Laramie, I swear I will. Just give me another chance.'

'Had your chance, Simpson. It's a falsehood that folks get second chances. Least in our line of work.'

'No . . . ' Simpson muttered, shaking harder. 'No, please, Drake. Please let me make this right.'

Drake peered at the man, the fury within him now cold liquor inebriating his soul. 'You should be on your knees when you beg me, Simpson. Only proper.'

Drake set a hand atop Simpson's head, pressed him down to his knees as his two men kept hold of each arm.

Drake watched the man a moment, fascinated by his fear, the way the small boy he had been used to watch small animals he captured and tortured before killing them fear him. Terror was a powerful musk, more potent than any bargirl's whispers, far stronger than the pathetic love a boy had once craved from a father who didn't give a damn, a father whom he had tracked down and murdered, though he had never told Bethany.

Simpson tried to look up, his eyes awash with tears, with supplication. It pleased Drake, surged through him like a drug.

His hand swept to the Smith & Wesson at his hip. It happened so suddenly Simpson never got the chance to scream. There was just crashing thunder the moment the muzzle pressed to his forehead, then the spray of bone and blood.

The two men holding his arms let go and Simpson fell face forward to the floor, lay still.

Drake peered at him a moment, the thrill of killing dissipating far faster than it used to. In a moment it was gone and all that remained was the cold rage always simmering in his belly.

'Get rid of him,' he said, then went back to the window and stared out at the black night.

5

Two hours dragged by like an eternity to John Laramie as he sat in the sawbones's waiting room. Every cell in his body urged him to try tracking the man who shot Bethany, but he had no way of doing so. The hardcase was long gone and finding any kind of trail in the dark was impossible. Even in broad daylight it would prove problematic, because of the foot traffic in the street and on the boardwalks. The man's tracks would be lost among dozens of others.

He had no place to start, no clues to follow, but he had a young woman fighting for her life. He reckoned it was at least some solace that the doc hadn't come out yet. That meant she was still alive and that was better than the alternative.

He came out of the hardbacked

chair, teeth clenched, every nerve crawling. The waiting was driving him stir crazy. He rubbed at the tension gripping the back of his neck, rolled his shoulders. She's still alive, he told himself again. That's all he could ask for right now. But he didn't delude himself. Gut wounds seldom turned out well. If that woman lived it would be some sort of miracle and he had long ago stopped believing in such things.

He went to the window, peered out into the dark night. Frost coated the edges of the glass, made him shiver slightly, though it was more from worry than any chill.

'How did that hardcase know I was at the saloon?' he muttered, running a finger over his lower lip. That he had known was certain, for Laramie was convinced the man had been waiting on him to come out of that room, not Bethany. Least, the odds were for it. If Lewis wanted his sister dead, she would have been by now, because it was obvious the outlaw knew she was in town.

That meant someone had informed Lewis while they were up in the room. He estimated he had been in there at least two hours, out cold for at least half that. Plenty of time for someone from the saloon to ride out and deliver the message, assuming Lewis was holed up somewhere in the vicinity. Lewis had sent a man back and everybody in the barroom must have seen the hardcase go upstairs. Yet no one had lifted a finger to stop him.

He gazed back at the closed door to the examination room. He could go back to the saloon now, question the barkeep and that redheaded dove, force one of them to tell him if anyone had left the bar. Once he had that person, he had a lead back to Drake Lewis.

He decided to wait, worry over Bethany's fate eating at his nerves too acutely. He'd pay a visit to the saloon tomorrow. The barkeep looked like the weakest link; he'd try him first and leave the dove till later. That girl, she appeared a hard one, someone used to keeping secrets she could later use for personal gain. But maybe enough greenbacks would loosen her tongue. He hadn't met a bargal who could turn down a passel of cash yet.

One thing was certain: Drake Lewis knew John Laramie was in town and had targeted him as a threat. Tonight's attempt on his life would not be the last. He'd neglected to ask Bethany just how many men were in the Cross Gang, but he guessed no more than four or five, from accounts he had read in papers. A small gang functioned efficiently, made fewer mistakes, and a man like Lewis would find leading a smaller bunch much easier. Too many might prove a threat in the long term — a slit throat while sleeping, or a bullet in the back. A man like that made enemies fast; he needed a few men he could trust or control through fear.

A sound came from the door as the handle turned and Laramie spun from the window. The doc, features haggard, grim, peered at him, sighed. He tossed something to Laramie and Laramie caught it. A bullet.

'I did the best I could, but she's in a bad way. She makes it through the next couple days she may pull through. The bullet missed her vitals but she lost a lot of blood. And of course infection is always a risk.'

Sinking guilt hit his belly. 'If I got her to you sooner . . . ?'

The doc shrugged, weariness in the expression. 'Hard to say. Doubt it would have made much difference, though. She's a strong one, I'll give her that. Not many, man or woman, would have survived what she's been through.'

'Reckon you don't know how accurate that is, Doc.' Laramie swallowed at the knot of emotion in his throat and remained silent for a moment. He wasn't a godly man but he said a small prayer for her. Hell, couldn't hurt and despite the short time he had known her he judged she would have wanted that. 'Can I see her?'

The doc frowned, raised his eyebrows. 'Won't do you any good. She's unconscious. I gave her enough laudanum to kill the pain of ten bullets.'

'Like to, just the same.'

The doc nodded, motioned with a hand. Laramie followed him into the examination room, noting the blood-soaked bandanna and clothes set aside on a table. A second door at the back of the room led to a small recovery room, sparsely furnished with a bed, bedside table upon which sat a low-turned lantern, porcelain pitcher, basin and drinking glass. A hardbacked chair occupied a corner, and a small dresser was against the north wall. The south wall had the only window and a threadbare carpet lay on the floorboards next to the left side of the bed.

Laramie moved past the doc, went to the bed and peered down at the young woman. Her face appeared unnaturally pale, but still an inner beauty shone through. He reached down, touched her cheek lightly with the back of his fingers, then brushed a stray chestnut lock from her face.

'I *will* find him, Bethany. He'll pay for what his man did. His man will pay, too. You got my word on that.'

Kill him, Laramie . . .

Rage surged through his being and he had all he could do right then to keep the darkness from swallowing him. It was getting more difficult to keep it at bay now anyway and the sight of the helpless woman lying in the bed, fighting for her very life . . .

'She needs rest, son,' the doc said, coming up behind him and putting a hand on his shoulder, drawing him from his dark thoughts.

Laramie nodded. 'I'll take care of any bills, Doc. Make sure she gets whatever she needs.' He turned, peered at the man, reading him, making certain this time he didn't leave her in the hands of someone who didn't give a damn. He saw compassion in the man's eyes, not fear.

'I'll do my best, son. But — '

'I know.' He paused, took a shallow breath. 'Why ain't you like the rest of them, Doc?'

'The rest of them?' The sawbones gave him a puzzled look.

'The townsfolk, I mean. They're all scared of the man who's responsible for this. None of them would lift a finger to help her.'

The doc turned away, plainly uncomfortable with the question. 'Best not to ask too many questions in this town right now, son.'

'But I reckon that's exactly what I have to do. I want the man who did this. I won't fear him.' He paused. 'You know anything about the Cross Gang?'

The sawbones jolted and Laramie knew he had hit a nerve. The older man turned back to him, conviction in his eyes. 'I know they come in here and take what they want and nobody does a thing to stop it. I'm an old man, son. I help folks when they need it and once I was forced to fix a flesh wound one of them got. But I don't ask questions or make trouble and they let me live, case they need me, I reckon.'

'But you helped her . . . ' Laramie ducked his chin to the bed.

The doctor licked his lips, hesitated. 'I took an oath; I couldn't just let her die. I have my limits and those limits end at letting another human being suffer or die without me doin' my best to try savin' them. They kill me for it, so be it. I've led a good life.'

Laramie smiled a lifeless smile, admiration for the older man filling him. 'You know where they go, where they hole up?'

The sawbones shook his gray-thatched head. 'No notion. They come and they go, mostly to the saloon. No one dares follow them. Leader stays mostly out of sight. Has his men threaten folks.'

'The man who shot her . . . he was likely aiming at me.'

The doc nodded. 'I figured as much. No reason to shoot this girl unless she got in the way accidentally.'

Laramie neglected to mention Bethany's connection to the gang leader. He didn't need to spook the sawbones anymore than likely he had already. 'You know who I am?'

'I recognized ya . . . '

'Then you know what I do.' Laramie stepped towards the door, muscles tightening at the thought of Drake Lewis. 'Whatever happens, you take care of that girl.'

The doc, not turning, nodded. 'I will, Mr Laramie. Or die trying.'

* ★ ★

John Laramie slammed the door to his hotel room and pressed his back against it, fighting the waves of rage that burned through his body like wildfire. The sight of Bethany Lewis lying in that bed, helpless, barely clinging to life, kept prying at his mind. Images of the night's events flashed through his thoughts, too, and he saw her being struck by the bullet, falling to the floor, blood pooling on her belly.

You have to kill him, Laramie! It would be so easy. Let the darkness take over.

'Nooo!' he yelled, shoving away from the door. His arm lashed out, hurling a pitcher of water and a porcelain washbasin from the top of the bureau. They hit the wall, rebounding to the floor. The pitcher shattered, water splashing across the worn wooden floor in an inkblot pattern that reminded him of spilled blood. He whirled, slammed a fist into the wall, which was covered with foiled red-striped papering. The papering was peeling in places, stained with god-knew-what in others. The room was tiny, typical as they went in these parts. Just a bed, nightstand with a lantern, a couple chairs against the opposite wall.

His heart pounded, beating a throbbing accompaniment inside his skull. Sweat streaked from his forehead, streamed down his face.

Give in, Laramie! You know you

want to. You've been fighting it too long. It's who you are, who you'll always be. Let the darkness take control. Kill Drake Lewis. He deserves to die for what he's done.

No, dammit! He hadn't wanted this. He had come to Lancerville looking to hide from his past, from the dark force threatening to overwhelm him and turn him into a something no better than the monsters he chased down. The dark thing inside him had struggled to break free for years, and at times he had almost welcomed it. Now it had grown too strong, and if he killed again, there would be no return.

You have no choice, Laramie. You have to avenge that girl. You can't let that bastard kill more innocent folks.

If he killed Lewis the way he had some others there would be no turning back, no retiring, no more running from what he was becoming. An avenger, a man who executed the guilty, without remorse or regret. How could he live with that? How would he live with himself?

A memory blazed in: four years ago in Dallas, the first time he recollected feeling the killing fever course through his veins. It had raged like white-hot fire, a bloodlust that could never be completely satiated.

Justice. That's what he had called it when he shot that man point blank. He could have brought him in, but the hardcase had murdered a young woman and her child in a bank robbery. Laramie had tracked him down, driven by fury and a righteous sword of rationalized duty. When he found the outlaw he'd confronted the man, told him to go for his gun, though he knew it was merely an excuse to put lead in him. Not justice, simply execution. And oh, how good it had felt. Good enough to scare the living hell out of him but not frightening enough to stop him. Like an addiction hungering to be fed, he'd needed more, craved it.

Other 'executions' came after that.

Men too vicious to let live, all guilty of reprehensible crimes, though cowards when it came down to their own deaths. It was amazing how easy it became, forcing the act of impotent self-defense upon those men, pulling the trigger. Like a living dark force that locked away all sympathy and compassion. As though he were apart from himself, merely a lost observer, the man he was fading a bit more with every kill.

But something within him had rebelled just before the darkness devoured him completely, some shred of morality, humanity. He'd fought what he was becoming, grappled with ever-increasing guilt over his deeds. He'd stood at the edge, hands bloody, soul bloodier, a step away from an abyss of perpetual, thinly justified murder.

To many men the notion of killing hardcases who deserved it wouldn't have mattered. But to John Laramie it meant a choice, Heaven or Hell. And once the decision was made, there would be no turning back.

Somehow he had to find a way to bring in Drake Lewis, let the law deal with him.

You'll have no choice; Lewis will never come peaceably.

No, he wouldn't. If the outlaw forced a confrontation, it would be kill or be killed. But that was different. It wasn't execution. It was self-defense.

Again rage coursed through him and he hammered a fist against the wall, then hit it again and again until blood ran between his fingers and smeared the paper. His breath beat out in hot jerky gasps.

A knock sounded on the door and he barely heard it. It came again and his head lifted. He dragged his forearm across his brow, mopping away sweat. His eyes focused on the small room.

'Mr Laramie?' a voice came from beyond the door. The hotel man. 'You all right? Man in another room said he heard banging coming from your room.'

Laramie took a deep breath, steadying himself. 'Yeah . . . yeah, I'm fine. Bumped into somethin'.' It sounded like a lie but he didn't give a damn. 'Need a new pitcher and basin, though.'

'We don't need any trouble, Mr Laramie,' the hotel man said, voice tentative.

'It's . . . all right. You won't get any.' He waited, and after a moment the hotel man's footsteps receded down the hallway.

Laramie went to his saddlebags, which were draped over the end of the bed. He drew out a clean bandanna and mopped the blood from his knuckles, then tossed it on the nightstand. They were skinned, but that would not bother him; he was used to hitting things.

He had no choice but to find Lewis and what happened when he did . . . well, it happened. He would have to find a way to keep his word to Bethany and hold on to his sanity at the same time.

In the meantime he was in no mood to sit in his room, waiting. He knew sleep wouldn't come easy and he would only be tormented by nightmares after the night's events. He had intended to question the barkeep and dove tomorrow, but he reckoned now was as good a time as any. And it might give him an excuse to hit something softer than a wall.

*　*　*

That the barkeep was none too happy to see him was obvious the moment John Laramie stepped into the saloon. The hour had gotten late and only a half dozen cowboys remained, but they were a seedy lot, and included those who had been casting him an eye earlier in the evening. They knew him, knew what he did, what he was and they wanted no part of him in this town.

'What the hell you doing back here?' the barkeep said, stepping around to the front of the counter. He had grabbed a shotgun, clutched it in white fingers in one hand.

The redheaded bargal was at the end of the bar, sitting on a stool, peering at him with a peculiar, almost humorous look. She gave him an odd little smile that said something he couldn't put a finger on. Two other men watched him as he came down the three steps to the barroom proper.

Laramie's cold gray eyes locked on the barkeep. 'You best put that shotgun down, 'fore you find you need the doc to extract it from your ass-end.' His hand slipped to the handle of the Peacemaker at his hip.

The 'keep didn't move for a moment, his dull blue eyes darting. Apparently he thought better of challenging the manhunter and eased the shotgun up, then set it on the bartop.

'She die?' the redhead asked, a small giggle escaping with her words.

'Shut the hell up, Lily,' the 'keep said, casting her an acid glance. The man was afraid of John Laramie, that was plain, but he had no such qualms when it came to a woman.

'Jesus, Bill, just askin',' she said, the little smile back on her lips. 'Man looks all shook up, don't he? She musta done died. Do believe he's got a thing for that ugly mattress-warmer.'

Laramie's gaze shifted to the woman, eyes narrowing. 'Like the man said, shut the hell up.' His tone brooked no argument but she seemed inclined to give him one just the same. She had laughed at the barkeep but something in her eyes told Laramie it was nowhere near as funny coming from the manhunter. Hate. Hate reflected from her eyes, not fear like the rest of the folks in this town.

'An' if I don't, Mr Manhunter?' she said, tone defiant, chin jutting forward. 'What you gonna do, hit me, maybe? Shoot me like all those awful outlaws you hunt down?' She punctuated it with a fake laugh that rode his last nerve.

His hand swept to his Peacemaker and in a blur it came up. Three shots, and bottles in a hutch behind the bar exploded under the impact of lead. Glass rained to the floor and liquor splashed the gilt-edged mirror on the wall beside the hutch.

'Judas Priest!' the 'keep said, face reddening. 'You can't just come in here and — '

Laramie swung the Peacemaker — hard. The gate clacked from the bartender's jaw with a thud and the man's eyelids fluttered. He went down beside the bar, half-sitting, half-lying, spitting blood.

The bargirl went silent, hate still glaring from her eyes. Laramie holstered the gun, bent over and, grabbing two handfuls of the man's shirt, hauled the 'keep back to his feet. Blood snaked from one corner of the bartender's mouth.

Laramie jerked the man's face close to his own. 'You listen and you listen good, you sonofabitch. One thing I don't abide is cowards, especially when their yellow-bellyin' gets innocent folks shot.'

The 'keep's eyes darted and his lips quivered. 'What do you want here, Laramie? We're just tryin' to survive.'

'So's a young woman who got gutshot earlier tonight. You're gonna tell me whatever it is you know about Drake Lewis and his gang.'

'I never heard that name!' the bartender said in a tone that was as close to a whimper as Laramie had ever heard from a man.

'You're lyin'.' Laramie hurled the man sideways. The 'keep went over a table, crashed to the floor. Rage took over and Laramie knew he was again close to embracing the darkness wanting him. He stepped towards the 'keep, intending to grab him again and force an answer from him.

Three cowboys had come out of their seats. One swung a half-full whiskey bottle at Laramie's head. Whatever fear Drake had put into them had to be powerful for them to risk taking on a man with Laramie's reputation.

Instinct saved the manhunter from

getting brained. He felt more than saw the bottle coming and ducked. It whisked over his head and in return his foot swept out, caught the man behind the knee. The man's leg buckled, went out from under him, and he came down hard flat on his back, a cloud of sawdust billowing around him. The bottle flew from his hand, rolling to a stop yards away.

Laramie got no time to survey his work. One of the two standing men threw a punch that took him square in the jaw. Pain stitched through his teeth and his senses reeled. He got an arm up to avoid a second blow, instinctively pistoning a fist at the man in answer.

The man flew backward as the fist crashed into his nose, pulping it in a spray of blood. He staggered and Laramie dove at him, launching an uppercut that lifted him off his feet and sent him to the floor.

The remaining cowboy grabbed him from behind, wrapping both arms about his chest and hoisting him off his feet. The man squeezed and Laramie struggled to breathe. He raked a bootheel backward along the man's shin and the cowboy let out a bleat, loosened his grip.

Laramie twisted, hammered the heel of his fist into the man's southern parts; his attacker suddenly released his hold.

Stepping back, Laramie whirled, avoiding a blow from the first cowboy, who had gotten back to his feet. The second man and the barkeep had regained their legs as well. The 'keep eyed the shotgun on the counter, made a move for it.

Laramie doubled, torso swooping under a lashing punch from the cowboy, then lunged at the bartender, getting between him and the weapon. He snapped a short right cross that put the man back on his britches, then flung the shotgun to the floor behind the bar.

The bargal watched in amused fascination, making no effort to intervene. Laramie glanced at her from the corner of his eye, making sure she made no move to help the others.

Two men charged him, blood running from their noses and lips. The first shot a fist towards his face. Laramie ducked right, fired a blow that caught the man in the breadbasket. The cowboy doubled, but before Laramie could finish him off the second man connected with a powerful left that sent him backward a step.

The man came forward, swinging. Laramie tried to duck but was still partly stunned. The blow glanced across his temple, and stars exploded before his eyes. He swung on instinct, hoping to connect, but missed. Another blow staggered him and he nearly went off his feet.

With a roar, he shook his head, vision snapping clear. He swung as the man lurched in for another blow, but some of the sting had gone out of his punch. He hit cheekbone but the man shook it off, hammered a fist into Laramie's forehead.

Laramie almost went down again. Apparently the man expected him to fall, because he paused to examine his work. That moment was all the manhunter needed. He hit the man square in the teeth, then hit him again, and again. The man staggered and Laramie drew back for a roundhouse.

'That will be quite enough, Mr Laramie.' A voice came from the batwings.

Laramie turned, head thrumming, heart banging, blood running from his own lip. The marshal stood in the doorway, gun in hand.

'Where the hell were you earlier tonight when that girl got shot?' Laramie said, spite in his voice.

The lawdog eyed him, irritation plain on his face. 'Time you and I had us a parley, I reckon. I need to force you to come along?'

Laramie shook his head, with a forearm swiped blood from his lip, then located his hat, which had come off during the fight. He cast the 'keep a poison glance. 'Wouldn't be surprised if you and I had us another meeting.'

The barman glared at him, but remained silent as Laramie left the saloon with the marshal.

6

'You've caused quite a ruckus in the short time you've been in town, Mr Laramie,' Marshal Sanders said as he closed the door to his office behind them. The office was small, with a bank of three empty cells along the back wall, a side door that opened into the alley, and a gun rack on the east wall. 'Have a seat.' The marshal indicated a hardbacked chair in front of the desk.

Laramie walked to the seat, lowered himself on to it, not bothering to remove his hat. 'Seems like I can't take all the credit for that ruckus, now, can I, Marshal? Somethin's been going on in this town for a spell, I reckon.'

The marshal, a man pushing fifty, with gray-dappled hair and muttonchop side whiskers that framed an angular face, went to a small table holding a blue-enameled coffee pot. He poured coffee into a tin cup, offered it to Laramie, who shook his head.

'You don't mind, I've learned to be a mite more careful what I drink in this town,' Laramie said.

The marshal gave him a perplexed narrowing of his eyes, then shrugged. He went to his desk, lowered himself into the comfortable chair behind it. After taking a sip of his coffee, he set the tin cup on the desktop, peered at Laramie.

'You've got quite the reputation, I hear tell. How many men you lay claiming to killin'?'

'Too many of 'em . . . ' Laramie said, not much in the mood to discuss his track record. 'But you ain't brought me here to discuss my reputation.'

The marshal sighed, ran a finger over his handlebar mustache. 'Why'd you come to this town, Mr Laramie? You come in lookin' for someone?'

'Only one I came in lookin' for was myself, Marshal.'

The lawdog's brow furrowed. 'Don't reckon I follow.'

'Was lookin' to retire. Figured Lancerville was just the sort of nice little town for a man to live out his golden years.'

'You're a long way from your golden years, Mr Laramie.' The marshal's tone said he didn't believe a word of Laramie's explanation. 'And men like you don't usually retire.'

Laramie uttered a lifeless chuckle. 'I've heard the speech . . . but it's the God's honest. I planned to leave manhunting behind me.'

'You picked the wrong town.' The marshal said it bluntly and a shimmer of fear danced in his blood-shot eyes. 'This ain't the place to settle. I don't reckon it ever will be.'

Laramie frowned. 'A man made me aware of that earlier tonight when he tried to kill me.'

'He shot a young woman.' The marshal offered it as if hoping Laramie would take the notion that the bullet hadn't been meant for him, but his tone didn't sell it.

'Her brother, Marshal. He runs the Cross Gang and I think you know it.' Laramie was tired of beating around the same bush. Bethany had indicated the marshal was less than reliable and it was time to push the man a bit.

'I don't know a thing, Mr Laramie, other than before you came in we had a peaceful town. Your kind only brings trouble and I reckon I'd like to ask you to be movin' on.'

A measure of irritation came back to Laramie's being. 'See, I can't do that, Marshal. I might let go the fact someone shot at me earlier tonight, because I want to get away from what I am. But an innocent woman might die because a man named Drake Lewis wanted me dead, just in case I was here to take him in, I figure. He threw the first punch. I aim to throw the last.'

The marshal's body went rigid, the answer plainly one the lawdog didn't want to hear. 'I could arrest you, Mr

Laramie. Or run you out.' A hitch came with the marshal's words.

'You could try.' Laramie stood, clutched the edge of the desk with both hands and leaned towards the marshal. 'But we both know you don't have the balls. Otherwise Drake Lewis wouldn't be comin' and goin' as he pleased and that girl wouldn't be fighting for her life.'

'Leave it alone. Mr Laramie.' The marshal's eyes grew hard, but fear still glared like twin skulls within them. 'Nothin' good will come out of you pokin' your nose into things.'

'You're a coward, Marshal, just like the rest of the folks in this town.'

'I want to live, I won't apologize for that.'

'So did the young woman. Fact is, she had the courage to try to help folks, way you and the rest of this town don't.'

'And look where it got her, Mr Laramie. Same place it would get us all. Leave it be. Ride out and forget you ever saw this place. You say you're lookin' to retire, be on your way and go through with it.'

Laramie straightened, disgust for the lawman welling. He had seen his share of crooked marshals in towns worse than this, but in his mind Sanders was worse; he was a man who wore a star made of paper.

'Too late for that, Marshal. You want to arrest me for somethin' you best be doin' it. Otherwise, I'm getting me an early start lookin' for a shooter.'

'Please, Mr Laramie. Whatever you think of me and the folks in this town, I'm beggin' you to just leave Lancerville. Let us live our lives.'

He uttered a humorless laugh. 'You really think Drake Lewis will let you all just go on like nothin' happened once he gets tired of this town? And make no mistake, Marshal, he will get tired of it soon enough. Once he's used it up he'll throw it away. His type always does. But he won't want to leave witnesses or any chance of a trail leadin' back to him.'

123

Fear strengthened in the marshal's eyes. He knew Laramie was right and the thought had likely crossed his mind a number of times. But he was trapped in a prison of his own making.

'You'll regret stayin', Mr Laramie. One way or the other. Tonight was some kind of omen. There's blackness coming and it's following you here.'

'Don't rightly believe in omens, Marshal. And that blackness ain't comin', it's been here all along. Look in the mirror, you'll see it.'

Laramie moved towards the door, paused with his hand on the handle. 'You know anything that will help me find this gang it's your duty to tell me. I won't take kindly to it if I find out you've been holding anything back.'

The lines in the marshal's forehead deepened. 'They call you Hell on Hoofs, Mr Laramie. You best pray that's more than some pulp writer's clever handle for you and live up to it, you go around talkin' way you have. And stay out of the saloon or next time I *will* throw you in a cell.'

Laramie smiled a thin smile. 'We'll see.' He stepped out into the night, closing the door behind him. The marshal, like the barkeep, was indeed hiding something. If he had learned one thing in his years on the trail it was reading men and the lawdog was as scared as the rest of the folks in this town. But was he scared enough to get blood on his own hands when it came down to it?

★   ★   ★

Ten minutes after John Laramie left the marshal's office the side door opened and Marshal Sanders damn near came out of his seat. Christ on a crutch, his nerves were just eaten up and the man who stepped through the door was the one responsible.

He tried to suppress a shiver but couldn't quite manage it. He was as scared as a man could be and he was ashamed to admit it. He'd never wanted this, never wanted his town to be in the grip of a murderous sonofabitch who gave a damn about nothing and no one. Things weren't supposed to have turned out this way. Lancerville had been a nice peaceful little town when he took over as marshal and that was how he had imagined it staying, until he retired. He had never reckoned on Drake Lewis.

But John Laramie was wrong in his assessment of him; oh, yes, he had seen the disgust in the man's gray eyes and he couldn't rightly blame the man-hunter. Hell, he disgusted himself. Laramie thought him pure coward. But that wasn't it, entirely. He was afraid of Drake Lewis and he did shield the outlaw, but it was much more than that. He had a wife, Hattie. God, how he loved that woman. She had given him thirty years of bliss and two fine sons. He was afraid for her. Lewis knew where to find her and had told him so. The outlaw had also informed him just what would happen to that woman should Sanders refuse to keep up his end of the bargain.

He believed Lewis. He knew the low-down bastard meant what he said and would not hesitate to murder her. The man's eyes were dead, utterly without anything human within them.

And no matter what hell Lewis put this town through, Sanders would not risk that woman's life.

A thin laugh, like demons chortling, shook him from his thoughts. Drake Lewis had reached the desk, was leaning on it with both fists.

'You look distressed, Sanders,' Lewis said in that ingratiating tone Sanders had come to loathe. 'Surely you aren't unhappy to see me.'

'What the hell happened tonight, Lewis? God in Heaven, your sister — '

'A mistake,' Drake Lewis said, a black cloud passing over his face. 'A mistake that has been rectified.'

'She's dying; I don't see how you call that rectifying.'

'She ain't your concern. John Laramie

is. What the hell did he want?' Lewis's tone had suddenly acquired an edge and Sanders knew he had stepped close to a line, one that would get him killed if he kept pushing it.

'He wants you, I reckon,' Sanders said, voice shaking a hair. 'He wouldn't leave. I told him to.'

Drake Lewis straightened, went to the window and peered out into the darkened street. 'I didn't reckon he would. Man like that don't back off. He ain't as cowardly as the folks in this town.'

The words stung, but the lawdog held his tongue on that point. 'His rep — '

'Is words on a page, Sanders. Nothing more. A self-righteous s-o-b who rides his own press. He come lookin' for me?'

A laugh escaped Sanders's lips. He couldn't help it as the irony of the question struck home.

The outlaw spun from the window, fury blazing like flaming death's heads in his green eyes. 'What the goddamn hell you find so funny?'

'Your man isn't the only one who made a mistake tonight,' the marshal said, before he could stop himself. 'Laramie came in lookin' to retire and settle down, Lewis. He wasn't looking for you or your gang. Least not until your sister got hold of him.'

The Smith & Wesson came from Drake Lewis's holster and leveled on Sanders in the space of a heartbeat. All expression dropped from the lawdog's face and he tried to press himself deeper into his chair, as though it would somehow make the impact of the bullet less deadly.

Drake Lewis held the gun on him, teeth clenched, tendons writhing on the back of his hand as he squeezed the handle.

A trickle of sweat wandered from the lawdog's brow down his face. He fought to keep his lip from quivering, a prayer that somehow if he died in the next moment Drake Lewis would leave his wife be going through his mind.

'You're goddamn lucky you still might have use left in you and I don't want the county sending another lawman in here right now.'

Sanders swallowed hard, nodded a jerky nod. 'Maybe ... maybe you should pull stakes, Lewis. Laramie won't quit, is all I'm saying.' He had to force the words out, because his heart pounded in his throat hard enough to stop all sound.

Lewis lowered the gun, holstered it. 'You'd like that, wouldn't you, Sanders? Like it if we just up and left. But, you see, I've taken a shine to your little corner of the West.'

'Lily?' The marshal let out a breath, his heart finally slowing.

'Till I get tired of her. That might be tonight, tomorrow, a week from now. Hard to tell with me.' Lewis paused, eyes narrowing on the lawdog. 'Why didn't you hold him? Would have made things a hell of a lot easier for me.'

'I-I couldn't,' Sanders said, hoping the lie didn't show.

'You really want to lie to me, Sanders?' Lewis moved closer to the desk. 'He attacked men at the saloon, busted up the place. Surely you could have made some charge fit.'

'Hell, I wasn't thinkin', that's all.'

'Oh, you were thinkin', all right. You just weren't thinkin' the right thing.' Lewis bent, pulled a Bowie knife from the sheath inside his right boot. He brought it up, let light from the lantern glint off the blade and flash across Sanders's face. Sanders's heart started pounding in his throat again, harder than it had before.

'Jesus, Drake, please — '

'You listen, lawman, and you listen good. Next time you get the chance to put him in a cell you best do it or I'll be payin' that little woman of yours a visit. She ain't a bad looker for her age, but I reckon you know that. Be a pity if those looks got messed up. You understand me?'

131

The marshal nodded, his voice suddenly gone. Oh, how he wished just this once he could stand up to the outlaw, put a bullet in him. But he couldn't. He couldn't risk anything happening to Hattie.

'Just so you don't go changin' your mind — ' Drake Lewis suddenly leaned in and grabbed the marshal's right wrist. He slammed the lawdog's hand on to the desk, fingers splayed. The marshal let out a bleat but the action came too fast for him to pull away. Lewis jerked the knife up with his right and brought it down with enough force to slice through bone.

* * *

'Been waitin' on you long enough, you sono-fabitch,' came the redhead's voice when Drake Lewis closed the door to the room above the saloon. 'Was expectin' you an hour ago.'

'Best keep your mouth in check, Lily,' he said, tossing his hat on to a hardbacked chair and stepping closer to the bed.

The redhead swung her legs off the bed, high-laced shoes hitting the floorboards with a thud, and stood, then went to him. She came up on her toes and kissed him deeply. Christ, she tasted like that god-awful rotgut the saloon served, and he pushed her away.

'I ain't in the mood.'

Her green eyes narrowed and her thin lips drew into a hard line. 'I'm glad that no-good bitch got what she got. She was gonna kill you, you stupid owlhoot. She was hirin' Laramie to do it for her if she didn't do it herself.'

'Shut your goddamn mouth!' His fist came up in a blur, driven by a rage that never quite seemed to satiate itself, no matter how many men he killed or how many women he bedded. Drake Lewis was a creature of fury, had been since the day he was born. He knew in his black heart there would come a day when that rage would be uncontrollable and he would not return from its black fever. Luckily for the girl before him today was not that day.

The back of his fist collided with her mouth and she flew backward and down. She hit the side of the bed, slid into a sitting position, one arm propped on the mattress. As she peered up at him with dazed eyes, a snake of blood ran from the corner of her lips. Then she began to laugh, a shrill defiant giggle that might have chilled any man other than Drake Lewis to the bone. The woman was as loco as any he'd ever come across, nearly as crazy as him. Maybe that was what fascinated him about her so much.

'You can do better than that, Drake,' she said, and spat a stream of saliva and blood at the floor. 'Or maybe you're just upset 'cause you won't be gettin' close to your sister no more — '

He stepped towards her, cocking his arm to back-hand her. His teeth came together and balls of muscle stood out on either side of his jaw.

She giggled again. 'Go on, Drake. Hit

me again. Harder. Big man loves to beat his whores, don't he? Bet you hit your sister like this right before you took her, didn't you?'

It was all he could do not to pull his gun and blow her head off. It took every last ounce of his willpower. She showed no fear of him, only mockery and it pissed him off. He'd make her fear him. Oh, yes, and as soon as she did . . .

He lowered his hand, bent and grabbed her arms. Hoisting her to her feet, he hurled her around and slammed her against a wall. 'I told you to shut the hell up! You hear me?'

She giggled again. 'Oh, Drake, you're getting me all riled up. You know I like it when you play rough.' She bit at his lower lip and he jerked his head back.

'You're pushin' your luck, Lily. One day soon I'm going to put a bullet in that skinny little ass of yours.'

She laughed, something dancing in her eyes he swore was insanity. This woman was dangerous in a way he had never encountered and until he figured out what scared her she would interest him — and live. Maybe.

'But this ain't the day, Drake. And maybe, just maybe, I'll get you first.'

He peered at her, eyes hard, heart harder. *No, Lily,* he thought, *you'll never get me first. Your time is just about up.*

'I want you to do somethin' tomorrow,' he said, voice lowering. 'You're gonna make sure that no-good lawdog helps you with it, too.'

'What you got in mind, Sugar?' She jammed her lips to his, and the taste of blood and whiskey assailed his tongue, but with it the musk of danger, wantonness. Lily would live out this night, he reckoned, but how many more was indeed a question . . .

7

'How is she?' John Laramie asked as the doctor motioned him into the waiting-room. Morning sunlight painted the world in shades of gold and melted the thick frost on the ground and window panes. The serenity of the new day belied the darkness that pervaded Lancerville and simmered within the manhunter.

He reckoned he hadn't slept more than an hour upon returning to his hotel room after his parley with the marshal last night. Each time he drifted off to sleep his dreams were riddled with the faces of the men he had killed and the haunting sounds of their pleas, and he would awake drenched in a cold sweat. The nightmares warned him he was close to the edge again, perhaps much closer than he had ever been.

Waking moments weren't much better.

He'd stared at a fly-specked dark ceiling, reliving in his mind the moment that bullet had hit the young woman. He should have been first out that door; the bullet was meant for him and by some perverted quirk of fate it had found another. More guilt for a man already carrying a passelful.

'Reckon there's been no change,' the doc said, face grim. He was still in his nightshirt and sleeping cap, but it didn't look as if he'd slept much, either. He was worried about Bethany and the fact that her lying in that back room might just attract the very man responsible for putting her there. Laramie couldn't rightly blame him, and, unlike the marshal, the sawbones was a man who had earned his respect. 'But that ain't necessarily a bad sign. Least, it's better than the alternative.'

Laramie nodded, following the sawbones through the examination room. 'All quiet here last night?'

The doc turned before opening the door to the back room. His face appeared to have aged a few years since last night. 'You expect it wouldn't be?'

Laramie shrugged. 'We both know who she is and who put her there. But reckon he'd have to give a damn about her to pay a visit, and with me in town the odds are remote of that happening.'

'I hope you're right, Mr Laramie.' The doc opened the door and stepped aside. 'Not too long, now, you hear?'

Stepping into the room, Laramie frowned. Sunlight arced in a golden shaft through the window, dust pirouetting within the room. It fell across the bed in a soft shimmering blanket that made Bethany Lewis appear almost angelic. He pulled a hardbacked chair over to the bed, sat. Hell, he wasn't even sure why he had come. He'd never been inclined to get attached to a woman. In his line of work it was an unnecessary and unfair risk. Any person he chose to become close to would be a target for men looking to take revenge or have leverage against him. A woman had no place in that life.

But it was more than that. At times he just wasn't sure he could hold back what he was becoming, wasn't sure he could stay that darkness inside, and it would take a strong woman to stand by him. He'd never met the likes. Until last night. Bethany Lewis was a strong woman, stronger than she thought, and she had proved it. In a way, she had saved his life last night, taking the bullet meant for him. If she lived through this, he would be inclined to spend a lot more time with her, maybe truly retire, way he had planned.

'Some things just can't be done alone,' he said, voice low, and touched her hand. Maybe retiring was one of them, and for damn sure going after her brother on her own was another.

He bowed his head, then let out a long sigh. Ten minutes passed before he arose and went back to the waiting room. The doctor had dressed, was preparing for the day's business.

'Mrs Tucker's boy come down with the collywobbles,' the doc said, a feigned smile in his lips. 'S'posed to be in today. Third time this week, in fact. I s'pect the tyke's gettin' into his pa's moonshine.' The doctor paused, peered earnestly at Laramie. 'Hopin' there won't be a risk treatin' him here.'

A plea came with the words: find Drake Lewis and make sure he didn't show up and put his patients at risk.

'Do my best, Doc. Just wish I had a place to start.' Laramie went to the door, opened it, then stood on the front porch in the warming day.

'Mr Laramie,' the doc said behind him.

Laramie turned his head, looked back over his shoulder. 'Yeah?'

'You might start with the redhead at the saloon.'

Laramie's brow narrowed. 'Somethin' you didn't tell me last night?'

The older man shrugged, gripped the edge of the door. 'Not certain, Mr Laramie. Just know when those men do come in she's right popular with the leader. Rumor, you understand, but maybe there's something there.'

Laramie nodded and went down the steps. 'Got a notion there just might be.'

As he walked back towards town, having left his horse at the livery, the sun rose higher and glazed the emerald pines and fir with blazing yellow. Browned fallen leaves crunched beneath his boots. The short trail gave way to the clapboard and brick buildings of Lancerville, and he reached a boardwalk near the saloon moments later.

The redhead. Something about her rang false and with what the sawbones had told him maybe there was a reason Lewis visited her that went beyond the usual ministrations of a bardove. It was possible the dove was just frightened, like the others in the town, and showing it in a strange way. If she wanted to remain alive she would do whatever Lewis told her, or he might just have picked her as his favorite while he was here. Which would also make getting anything out of her, if, indeed, she knew anything, a crap shoot. But for the moment it was his only lead and he would follow it.

He noted the saloon was closed; he knew from the previous day it opened in the late afternoon, so finding the girl might be a problem. He doubted the marshal would be forthcoming with that information, so that left him waiting.

He settled for a quick breakfast at the café: eggs and bacon, and a pot of Arbuckle's. He picked at his food but the coffee was welcome, cleared his head some. Running on little sleep, his muscles ached and felt leaden. Hell, maybe he *was* getting old, like he'd told Bethany.

After leaving the café he headed along the boardwalk towards his hotel. His gaze scanned the street ahead of him, then shifted to the rooftops, searching for any glint of sunlight off metal or any other indication of a bushwhacker. He doubted Lewis would attack him outright so soon after last night's failure, but couldn't be too careful. Lewis knew his reputation, and whether he believed it, the man thought Laramie was here after him and wouldn't chance another failure. He'd plan better this time, make sure Laramie was in a vulnerable position.

He stopped, a prickle of apprehension running through the hairs on the back of his neck. That manhunter's sixth sense, which had saved his life on the trail countless times. His gaze darted along the opposite boardwalk, then behind him, but he spotted nothing. A few folks were about, heading towards shops or the café, but none gave him a second look. In fact, they seemed eager to avoid any eye contact whatsoever. News of the shooting had traveled fast, he reckoned.

He started forward again, hand edging down towards his Peacemaker. He had spotted no one, but he was being dogged just the same. He felt it.

Question was, by whom? Perhaps he

had been wrong in his assessment that Lewis wouldn't send his killers after him in broad daylight and so soon after his sister's shooting. He was used to outlaws being cocky or pulling boneheaded moves, but from what Bethany had told him Lewis was craftier than the average owlhoot.

Or maybe he was just hotheaded enough to make another mistake.

Laramie stepped from the boardwalk into the street, preferring the openness of the rutted hard-packed thoroughfare. If he were attacked it would be between him and the bushwhacker, less likely to chance an innocent life. He needed no more guilt on his conscience.

He paused at a trough recently filled by rain. Leaning over, he splashed chilled water into his face, careful to keep it out of his eyes so he could covertly peer down the boardwalk.

There. Near the marshal's office, a flash of cloth darting into the alley. With only a glimpse he couldn't tell whether it was a man or a woman; it was more a motion than anything else.

He straightened. If whoever was following hadn't noticed him looking, he might be able to double back and surprise him, but he had another idea. The street angled to the right a few paces ahead. Let the stalker come to him.

Laramie went forward again, his stride easy, as if he were in no particular hurry to be anywhere, nor alarmed. He didn't look back again. If whoever was following him wanted to take a shot he would have likely done so by now. No, whoever it was had something else in mind.

He turned the corner where the town angled on to a right-hand street, suddenly stepping up his pace and slipping into a short alley next to the gun-smith. He pressed his back to the wall, waited, breath shallowing. Steps clomped on the boardwalk, coming closer, little effort being made to silence them. He readied himself.

A handful of seconds later, the

footfalls became muffled as whoever it was stepped off the boardwalk and came around the corner. The stalker was alert but unprepared for someone waiting for her. Laramie grabbed her arms, swung her around and shoved her up against the building wall.

'Mite early to be lookin' for company, isn't it, miss?'

The redhead glared at him but her face quickly softened. 'Was plannin' on approachin' you when you got to your hotel, Mr Laramie. It ain't like you think. I didn't come after you lookin' to talk you out of your money.'

He studied her, unable to read what lay behind her green eyes. The woman was a practiced liar, no doubt, used to hiding things and telling men whatever they wanted to hear.

'Seems to me you were bein' right careful not to let me see you.'

'You can let me go, Mr Laramie. I won't run.'

With a frown, he released his hold on her arms and stepped back. She straightened her frilly skirt and tugged up one shoulder of her low-cut blouse. In the daylight her face appeared much harder, lined heavily around the mouth and eyes, despite a liberal application of warpaint and kohl. She done her hair in tight ringlets that corkscrewed to either side of her face and it was plain her freckled nose had been broken at one time in the past. Her thin lips appeared swollen slightly, as if she'd been hit since he'd last seen her at the saloon the previous night.

'I was bein' careful not to let someone else see me, Mr Laramie. Not you.' She stepped away from the wall, walking a few steps deeper into the alley. He turned towards her, not expecting her to run, but ready just in case.

'Somebody like Drake Lewis?'

The name got a reaction, one of deep fear. Her eyelids fluttered and she wrapped her arms around about herself.

'He's a bastard!' she said, venom

lacing her voice. He couldn't tell if the emotion were real or not. And that irked him. He could read men, but women were another story. He plain did not have enough experience around them.

'Came to the same conclusion. Why don't you tell me something useful?'

She shuddered, lower lip quivering. 'He beat me last night after you left, Mr Laramie. I was his favorite. But he reckoned I was gonna help you after what happened to his sister.'

Laramie nodded, a sliver of hope taking him. But something about it seemed almost too good to be true. His manhunter's sixth sense was going off again, but he couldn't tell why quite yet.

'He came to the saloon last night?'

She nodded, eyes glassy with tears. 'Came in after the marshal took you away. Said he wanted to spend some time with me because he was all troubled over his sister gettin' shot. Took me upstairs and started hitting me. Look.' She pulled down the right shoulder of her blouse, exposing livid marks where fingers had dug in deep, bruising. 'He likes to hurt me, Mr Laramie. He likes to hurt everybody.' Her voice shook and he couldn't deny that a measure of sympathy welled for the girl, along with fury for Drake Lewis.

'You got any notion where he's hid out?' He wasn't quite ready to accept her act, but he'd play it through to see where it led.

'You gotta promise you'll protect me, Mr Laramie.' She took a step closer, a tear leaking from her eye. 'If he finds out I told you anything and you don't get him he'll kill me. I think he's gonna kill me anyway, 'fore he leaves town. I'm afeared, Mr Laramie. We all are in this town.'

'Tell me where he is. You're tellin' the truth, I'll see to it you're safe from him.'

She peered at him with tear-filled eyes, and a sly smile slipped over her lips. 'Was hopin' you'd be my hero, Mr Laramie. I so needed one.'

His manhunter's sixth sense suddenly strengthened. Something was wrong. The girl had been putting on an act the whole time.

'What do you want, miss — '

'Like I said, a hero, Mr Laramie,' the girl said, her smile widening and cunning washing into her eyes. 'A man like yourself. Ten years ago when I was thirteen and my pa saw fit to pass me around to some of his drunk friends, I needed you then, Mr Laramie. Too late now.' She giggled and suddenly tore the shoulder from her blouse.

'What the hell — ' he started, but the girl rushed forward, throwing her arms about his waist and clinging to him.

'Oh, Mr Laramie, please don't hurt me, I'll do whatever you want, I swear I will.' Her voice came shrill and panicked, loud enough to carry far beyond the alley. He tried to thrust her away but she clung to him like leech.

'Get the hell off me,' he said, trying

151

to pry her loose. Her nails dug into his back.

'No, let me go!' she screamed.

'Mr Laramie . . .' A voice came from behind him and suddenly the girl let go, stepped back. Tears were coming from her eyes again and she clutched at the swatch of torn cloth at her shoulder.

'I was gonna give him what he wanted, Marshal,' she said, her voice shaking. 'He wouldn't stop tearing my clothes and wanting it right here.'

Laramie spun. Sanders stood at the opening of the alley, his gun drawn, left hand shaking as he aimed. That was bad, Laramie reckoned. A nervous man made stupid mistakes, pulled the trigger before thinking. The marshal's right hand was bandaged, a browned patch of dried blood where it was plain the pinkie finger was missing.

'She's lying, Marshal,' he said, keeping his voice level, eyes locking with the lawdog's.

The marshal's gaze flicked to the girl, then back to him. 'Don't look that way to me. Looks like you were manhandling her from where I'm standing.'

Sanders was lying, plain and simple. His voice shook as hard as his hand. Laramie might have had trouble reading the bargirl but he had no trouble reading the lawman. He had been set up and he had a notion why. Lewis wanted him where he would make an easy target, where he'd be defenseless. No better place for that than in a cell at the marshal's office.

He considered going for his Peacemaker. He was fast, and might take a nervous man by surprise. The marshal would pull the trigger but his aim was questionable. But that meant Laramie would have to kill him, and a seed of doubt told him the man was doing this out of fear, not criminal intent.

'She's working with Lewis, Marshal,' he said, knowing it would do him little good. 'That what you're doin'? Makin' me a sitting duck for a killer?'

Sanders's gaze dropped, guilt reflected in his eyes, then came back up. 'Appreciate it if you'd drop your gunbelt, real careful-like. Then we can all go back to my office and sort this out.'

Laramie frowned, hand easing to his buckle. He unhooked it, let the belt drop to the ground. The girl swooped down, picked it up, then ran to the marshal's side.

The lawdog motioned with his gun and Laramie began walking. The dove cast him a secret smile as he went past her.

8

Drake Lewis sat at the small table in the cabin, fire-ants of impatience biting at his nerves. He didn't like the fact he hadn't seen that damn dove all day; she should have reported in about Laramie's arrest by now. Went on much longer, he'd be inclined to think something had gone wrong again. But that whore was wont to go with her own mind, and as far as he was concerned that was a damn poor trait in his line of work.

Fact was, he suddenly didn't like a lot of things about this town. He'd made mistakes, and lately it was getting harder to think rationally. He was becoming more and more like his old man and that stuck in his craw. He had hated that sonofabitch, hated him more now for making him the way he was. But it wasn't entirely the old bastard's fault, was it? Lewis blood was just bad.

That was the only reason Bethany had shown any strength at the last. She wasn't a true Lewis and by some quirk of his nature he had decided to leave her alive, give her a chance. It wasn't compassion for what he had put her through, for he had none, not for her, not for anyone. It was more a morbid fascination with her suffering. He knew one way or the other she would come after him eventually. She had to. He had used her up, controlled her with fear. He had to admit, she surprised him, getting it in her damn fool mind to come kill him. He'd reckoned she would cave, become like him, want to join up willingly. He would have killed her, then. He didn't respect weakness in any form. Not after his pa had beaten it out of him.

But she had met Laramie, whether by design, accident or fate, and now he had other problems, ones he hoped to deal with, if that no-good whore ever got back here.

Whatever the case, he had come to a decision about Lancerville. With Laramie's death things would get too dangerous for him. No way the law was going to let a man with his rep just die easy. They would investigate and before long have a name to put a rope around.

He sighed, agitation increasing. He'd come to hate sitting around this abandoned mining cabin, come to hate it with a passion. The times he snuck in to see Lily and spend the night in her bed were no longer enough diversion. He had been careful, letting his men put the fear into this town, keeping his own face, and name, out of reach as much as he could. But there were those who could connect him with the Cross Gang, and that had to be rectified.

He fished in a breast pocket, pulled out a pack of papers. After tearing one off, he returned the pack to his pocket and dug out a small pouch of tobacco. He set the paper on the table, poured a measure of the tobacco on to it.

A sound caught his attention, hoof-beats, distant but approaching, and he looked up. Cleves stood at the window, while Jones sat on his bedroll, reading one of those damned dime novels that went on about men like John Laramie.

'Who is it?' he asked, voice low, dark.

'Lily,' Cleves said, frowning. 'What's she doin' comin' out here?'

Drake tucked the pouch back into his pocket. 'I told her to come once she did what I wanted. She's goddamned late.'

'What'd you want her to do?' Jones asked, looking up from the dime novel.

'You'll find out soon enough.' Drake rolled the tobacco in the paper, licked the edge. He stuck the cigarette into his mouth, fished in his pocket for a match. Snapping it to flame on a tooth, he set the end of the cigarette alight, took a deep drag, and tossed the match to the table.

A moment later the hoofbeats stopped outside the cabin. The door opened and the redhead stepped inside, that defiant smirk he had come to hate riding her lips. His gaze raked her, and she halted, as if thinking better about running her mouth, then moved over to the table and sat in the opposite chair.

'Where the hell you been?' he asked, blowing out a stream of smoke. 'You were s'posed to take care of that business I set you to hours ago.'

She giggled and his agitation clicked up a notch. 'Miss me, Sugar?'

He leaned forward, eyes narrowing, a dark rain moving across them. 'I asked you a question. I best get an answer before I decide to get me a new whore.'

She appeared ready to respond in kind, but after locking gazes with him apparently exercised one of her rare moments of restraint. She could consider herself lucky. He would have put a bullet into her if she hadn't.

'Marshal held on to me a while,' she said, voice hard. She was lying. He could tell. His gaze lifted to the window. Beyond, deep dusk had settled. He looked back to her. Her eyes were dull, hollow. Laudanum.

'Got a notion you needed some time sobering up,' Drake said. 'You should have come here first.'

She wrapped her arms about herself in a defiant gesture. 'I ain't workin' on your timetable, Drake. I took care of what you wanted. Figured I deserved myself a reward after.'

It took an effort not to kill her right then and there. But he reckoned that would ruin the fun they were going to have later tonight, before he rode out.

He looked at Cleves, then Jones, who had gotten up when Lily entered. 'We're movin' out later tonight.'

'What?' Lily said, shock hitting her face. 'What the hell you mean you're movin' out? I took care of Laramie. He's in the marshal's jail.'

Drake took another drag on his cigarette, letting the smoke fill his lungs, holding it, then blowing it out. 'Once Laramie's dead all sorts of law's going to come in here. I don't aim to be around when it does. Ain't many who

160

know my name and I aim to stay off the end of a rope.'

Anger burned the laudanum haze from her eyes. 'Marshal knows your name. Wouldn't be surprised if he even knows you're in this cabin.'

'He don't unless he followed you here.' His tone darkened, laced with accusation. ''Sides, our good friend the marshal's outlived his usefulness.' He shot a glance at his two men, who nodded.

'Barkeep knows it, too. He's seen you. Couple cowboys might have seen you sneak up, too.'

Drake shrugged, knowing she was right. 'They're too scared to say anything, but I reckon the barkeep's accident prone.'

'There's another who knows.' A vile implication rode her tone, and it irritated the hell out of him. He didn't like his mistakes being pointed out. Not one lick.

'She's dying,' he said, stubbing out the cigarette on the table. The smoke had suddenly become acrid in his nostrils, the taste bitter.

'She might live, Drake.' A sneer came to her lips and her tone. 'She might wake up and tell folks, way she told Laramie. She'll want to kill you even more now. You got to kill her.'

His hand snapped out like a snake snatching a mouse and grabbed her wrist. He squeezed and a small cry of pain came from her lips, chasing away the sneer. His two men looked on, eagerness in their eyes. No doubt they wanted a chance with her, but some whores he kept exclusive and Lily was one of them.

'She's to be left alone, you hear me? She's dying and she won't wake up.'

'You don't know that.' The girl's tone was snide, showing little fear. He hated the way that affected him, made him want her. He had hoped to make her fear before he left. But time had run out.

'Ain't your concern. You go back to town and wait for me later tonight. I'll come see you 'fore I go.'

'I'm goin' with you.' She tried to pull her wrist free, but he held it fast. His eyes drilled into her and he waited a moment, then released her, leaving a livid ring about her wrist.

'The hell you are. I'm not like to be dragging around a useless whore.'

Anger flared in her eyes and her face reddened. 'You best change your mind about that.' The threat in her tone was unmistakable. She stood, strode for the door. Cleves and Jones started to block her path but Drake gave them a shake of his head, telling them to let her go.

'You need me, Drake,' she said, pausing at the door. 'You know it. You best take me with you.' She opened the door, stepped outside, then slammed it behind her.

Drake stared at the closed door a moment, Cleves and Jones unmoving, awaiting orders. Lily was right: another knew his name in this town, one who wasn't afraid to speak it out of spite. *She* knew.

And that was one whore too many.

9

'What's he got on you, Marshal?' John Laramie asked from a cell at the back of the lawdog's office. He sat on the edge of the bunk, hands gripping the mattress, fingers white as they dug in. Outside the sun had set and the marshal got out of his chair to light a lantern, then went to the coffee pot and poured himself a cup.

'Reckon I have no notion who you are talking about, Mr Laramie. I also reckon I asked you nicely to leave last night and you plain refused. I'm inclined to make that offer again — coffee?' Sanders held out the tin cup.

Laramie shook his head. 'My answer hasn't changed. I aim to see Drake Lewis at the end of a rope.'

'You aim to get yourself killed,' Sanders said, going back to his desk and lowering himself into his chair. On the desk were the remains of his beefsteak dinner, which he'd only picked at. Laramie knew that more than the fact that he wouldn't leave Lancerville was troubling the man.

'You know I'm sitting here makin' a perfect target for him.' Laramie drilled the man with his gaze. A shadow of guilt passed over the lawdog's worn features. The man's face appeared older than it had last night and his once-broad shoulders sagged with the weight of unvoiced conscience. Sanders knew Laramie was right and it was preying on his mind.

'You're safe enough,' he said, picking up his fork and poking at cold fried potatoes, but his voice bled doubt. 'Till we get this charge sorted out,' he added without the slightest conviction.

'Lily's workin' with Drake Lewis and so are you.'

Sanders started, averted his gaze. 'Please, Mr Laramie . . . let it go.'

Laramie stood, coming to the bars, gripping them. 'I can't, Marshal. Not with that young woman lying in a bed at the doc's, dying. She deserves better than that. I made her a promise and I'll die keeping it.'

'You most likely will,' the marshal said, voice lowering, heavy. He poked at a piece of steak, then set down his fork. His gaze went to the window at the front of the office, as if he had heard something. He was antsy, Laramie noticed, was expecting something he wanted no part of.

'What is it, Sanders? They comin' for me?' Laramie kept his tone even, accusing.

'It's nothin', Mr Laramie. Just some cowboy walking on the boardwalk towards the saloon, I reckon.'

'What are you afraid of, Marshal? Drake Lewis, that much is obvious. What's he got on you? What does it take to make a lawman do an outlaw's bidding?'

Sanders's face reddened. He remained silent for long moments, shifted in his chair. He touched the star on his breast, finger tracing its points and valleys.

'Used to have a notion this stood for something, Mr Laramie. Long time ago when I first pinned it on. But a peaceful town . . . laziness sets in, complacency. You figure all those dreams you had of saving the West were just dreams and nothing more. Fact is, it's mostly routine and you sit around collecting your paycheck. Then you start hoping those dreams you had never come true, least not the part where you got to risk your hide. Man like you wouldn't know about that, I reckon.' He glanced at Laramie, a distant look now in his eyes.

'I reckon I came into your town lookin' for just what you're describin', maybe telling myself the same lies. Running from who I am.'

'I ain't runnin', Mr Laramie. I accepted who I am a long time ago. I just wanted to finish out my workin' days existin'.'

'Then Drake Lewis showed up . . . ?'

The marshal shrugged. He peered at his bandaged hand, lines on his brow deepening. 'Got one thing in the world that means a damn lot to me, Mr Laramie. My wife, Hattie.' The sag in the lawdog's shoulders became more pronounced.

Laramie saw the truth then. Drake had threatened the man's wife, giving Sanders little choice but to go along with whatever he wanted.

'He do that to your hand?' Laramie asked.

Sanders winced, telegraphing the answer.

'A reminder,' he said, after a moment. 'It's a good thing I'm left-handed.'

'Let me out of here, Marshal. If you know where Drake is, tell me. I can protect your wife.'

'Way you protected Bethany Lewis?' As the lawdog pinned Laramie with a damning gaze, a spike of guilt drove into the manhunter's belly.

'I didn't get the chance, Marshal. Didn't know fully what I was up against or expect Lewis would know I was coming after him.'

'And now you know what you're facin'?' Little confidence came in Sanders's tone. He picked up his tin cup, took a swallow.

'I'm aware of how he's plannin' to strike. You know Lewis or his men are going to come for me, kill me while I'm defenseless here. When they do, you'll have blood on your hands.'

'Dammit, Laramie!' The marshal suddenly hurled his coffee cup across the room. It hit the wall, ricocheted to the floor, where it rolled to a stop. Coffee splattered the wall, dripping down like browned blood. 'I'm a coward, Mr Laramie, all right? I know I am. But I won't risk Hattie's life on a chance you might succeed.'

'You're risking it anyway, Sanders.' Laramie locked gazes with the man again, gray eyes as hard as granite. 'When Drake Lewis decides to move on, he won't leave loose ends behind. You know who he is and he won't take a chance on you tellin' any other lawman his name, or someone like myself. He might kill Hattie, too, just because his type enjoys killin'.'

The marshal sighed, stood, leaned heavily on his desk. His face said he believed every word the manhunter had told him, despite his denials. 'I'm sorry, Mr Laramie. I just can't take that chance. I reckon along with bein' a coward I'm also a damned fool. Hattie's all I got, and if I die tomorrow, it'll be OK as long as she don't go first.'

'Hers and your own aren't the only lives you're risking. There's innocent folk out there he's killed, women he's raped. He'll go on doin' it if you don't find some balls, Sanders.'

'Well, if he does kill me I won't have it long on my conscience, will I?'

'Won't you? That the way you want to go out? Knowin' you're aiding a killer?'

'Please just shut the hell up, Mr Laramie. This is bad enough without you pointin' out my sins. I reckon you got plenty of your own. You'd have just moved on and settled like you told me, we wouldn't even be having this conversation.'

Laramie shook his head, looked down, then back to the marshal. 'A young woman made me realize sometimes we gotta risk fightin' the darkness. You got a lot to lose; I reckon I understand that all too well. But you made a choice when you pinned on that badge. Those innocent folks Lewis killed and will kill in the future, they never got a choice the way you and I did.'

A sound came from outside, the muffled beat of hoofs, and a sinking sensation hit John Laramie's belly. His manhunter's sixth sense set the hairs on the back of his neck tingling.

The marshal moved to the window. 'Christ on a crutch,' he muttered.

'It's Lewis, ain't it, Marshal? Comin' for me, way I told you he would. Way you knew he would the moment you were asked to keep me in this cell.'

The lawdog looked back to him, a pained expression on his face. 'His two men. Had three, but he told me the other was . . . gone, more or less.'

'You saw Drake last night?'

'He stopped by after you left. His woman came in first thing this morning, told me what I was to do. Said she saw you go into the café after comin' from the direction of the doc's and she was goin' to follow you when you left. I was to watch until the proper time.'

'How far away are they?'

'They just rode into town . . . 'bout halfway down the street now.'

'Comes down to a choice again, Sanders. Make the wrong one and you condemn innocent folks, take their choice away.'

'I . . . I . . . ' The lawdog's mouth opened, then closed. His Adam's apple bobbed and sweat broke out on his brow.

'You know they're comin' to kill me. They do, you got no hope of livin' through this.'

Outside, the hoofbeats drew nearer, like the banging of a death drum.

The marshal's head dropped and he seemed to deflate. 'I got no hope anyway, now, Mr Laramie. Reckon I had none from the day Drake Lewis came into this town.'

The hoofbeats came to a sudden stop. The silence that followed rang like a death knell.

Laramie clutched the bars tighter, hands going white with strain. 'Marshal . . . ' he said, voice rising.

The lawdog went to a set of keys hanging on a wall peg. 'You promise me, Mr Laramie. You promise me you will do your damnedest to protect Hattie from them if I don't survive this.' His old eyes searched Laramie's.

'You got my word.'

The marshal nodded, a mechanical expression, then lifted the keys from the peg and tossed them to Laramie. The manhunter caught them, unlocked the cell door and flung it open.

Boots clomped on the boardwalk beyond the door. Laramie's heart jumped, adrenaline pumping into his veins. The marshal had stashed his gun in a desk drawer, but he had run out of time. He whipped to a spot behind the door, pressed his back against the wall. The marshal stood frozen as the door started to open, his hand resting on the handle of his Colt, his face bleached.

Cleves came in first. Laramie hammered a fist to the side of the hardcase's head and the outlaw stumbled inward. The manhunter gave him no time to recover. He grabbed the outlaw, swung him around and slammed him into the wall. Cleves tried to throw a punch but Laramie's knee came up, burying itself in the man's crotch.

Cleves doubled over, groaning. Laramie delivered an uppercut that nearly broke his hand and lifted the man off his feet. Cleves dropped to the floor, unmoving.

Sanders wasn't so lucky. Jones had stepped in behind Cleves, reacted the instant he had seen Laramie hit his partner. The outlaw drew as Sanders tried to pull his own gun out of its holster. But he was old, slow, unpracticed from years of sitting behind a desk.

Jones pulled the trigger before the marshal got his gun halfway out of the holster. The crash of gunfire in the small room pounded against Laramie's eardrums. Lead punched into the marshal's chest, hurling him backward. He slammed against his desk, eyes wide, mouth gaping, then went down, his gun tumbling to the floor.

The outlaw swung his gun towards Laramie. The manhunter grabbed the blue-enameled coffee pot from the table, flung it at the shooter, top open. Scalding coffee splashed the man's face and he let out a screech, squeezing the trigger of his Smith & Wesson at the same time.

The shot went wide, the gun jerking from his grip. The coffee pot had hit his face hard, bounced off. He stumbled a step backward, pawing his eyes.

Laramie lunged for him, swinging a fist. With a crack nearly as loud as the shot, the man's nose became a flattened pulpy mass, spraying blood.

Another blow staggered the outlaw. Laramie stepped in, planning to give him no time to recover, but Jones suddenly fell forward, blindly clutching at the manhunter's waist. Laramie tried to sidestep, but the outlaw managed to wrap both arms around the manhunter's middle and force him off balance.

They both came down hard, the hardcase's arms beneath Laramie breaking the fall some. A brittle snap sounded, one of the outlaw's wrists breaking, and Jones started shrieking.

Laramie thrust the hardcase sideways, pounding the side of his head with a fist as he did so. The outlaw went silent, rolled on to his back.

Breath beating out, heart thundering, the manhunter came to his feet.

Behind him, Cleves had recovered and reached his feet as well, legs shaking. Clumsy fingers tried to get the gun out of his holster.

Laramie pivoted, sent a bootheel into

the man's ribs. Bone cracked and the man flew backwards, slammed into the wall. Laramie caught him with a right cross on the rebound and Cleves dropped, unconscious.

Taking no time even to catch his breath, the manhunter dragged Cleves into the cell he had formerly occupied, then followed suit with Jones. After locating the keys on the floor, he closed the cell door, locked it and flung the ring on to the marshal's desk.

He went to Sanders, knelt. A round hole surrounded by an ever-expanding areola of crimson showed in his chest. The lawman's breath came ragged, liquidy. The doc would have no chance of saving this man, no matter how fast Laramie got him there.

The marshal's arm came up and he gripped Laramie's biceps. 'Please . . . Hattie . . . '

Laramie nodded. 'I won't let anything happen to her, Sanders. She'll know you went doin' what was right. You ain't the coward you thought you were.'

'C-cabin . . . outside of town . . . old mining cabin . . . south end . . . Black Hill . . . '

'Drake's there?'

Sanders coughed blood, speckling his lips. He tried to nod. 'Tell Hattie . . . tell . . . I love . . . ' His eyelids fluttered and his head lolled back. Laramie gently lowered it to the floor.

Kill them. They did this.

His gaze went to the two unconscious outlaws in the cell. They were murderers. It would be so easy to give in to the darkness, put bullets in those men. He wanted to. Lord, how he wanted to.

He rose to his feet, for the moment in the grip of a blood fever that burned like hellfire in his veins. He went to the desk, pulled out the drawer and lifted his gunbelt. After strapping it on, his hand drifted over the butt of his Peacemaker, a chilled numbness moving through him.

It would be so easy, Laramie. Just give in. They deserve to die for what they did.

No. Those men would hang. He had the marshal's body as evidence and likely there were posters on those two somewhere. He could call in the county marshal to handle it. Right now, he had Drake Lewis to deal with and a promise to keep to a young woman lying in the doc's bed. The darkness would have to wait.

10

If that low-down sonofabitch thought he was just going to up and leave, he had another think coming!

Lily's eyes narrowed and her face hardened as she crept from the edge of the wooded trail towards the side of the sawbones's place. She could read Drake Lewis as easy as she could read any man, whether he thought so or not. When he met her later tonight it would be for the last time, to his way of thinking. She saw the death sentence in his eyes and she wasn't just another stupid whore. She knew his name and had threatened him, and he knew it. And planned to see to it she didn't live to tell anyone.

She uttered a low giggle, bending double as she made her way to a window from which buttery light spilled on to the frosty ground. Drake Lewis was used to using his women, then killing them. She'd known it the moment she laid eyes on him and something about the notion tickled her. She'd done it to a fella or two she used and robbed over the years herself. He was a challenge, a danger, a drug. She had never really expected him to take her with him when he left, and she didn't give a damn. What she wanted from him was the excitement, the risk of the shadow of death looming over her each time he came to her room, and the pleasure of killing him herself.

She hadn't felt so exhilarated in years. Any thrill from run-of-the-mill cowboys and outlaws or at the bottom of a laudanum bottle had run dry ages past. She recollected the fear rushing through her veins, the terror caressing her heart the day her pa had given her over to those men the first time. She'd been searching for that elusive feeling ever since, never quite finding it — until Drake Lewis rode into town. He was different from the rest. Diseased.

Without a lick of compassion for man or beast, except for that traitor sister of his'n.

Why he'd let her go on livin', Lily had no idea. Maybe it meant, in some way she couldn't rightly figure, that that tramp meant something to him.

She spat, sickened by the thought of him with her. She did have her limits, though many a man would have claimed no one had ever come close to finding them. But his sister? Even if they weren't related, it was . . . unnatural.

Another giggle escaped her thin lips and she blew out a stream of vapor. The moon had crept over the trees, glazing the frost-coated ground with alabaster and outlining her face in icy relief. The air held a chill, but she barely noticed. Fever was running through her veins, the fever of a coming kill, and the anticipation of what it would do to Drake when she told him later tonight what she had done, the look on his face as he breathed his last.

'Leave me behind, will you, Drake Lewis,' she muttered, voice as cold as the night air. 'I don't think so.'

She edged up to the house, beside the window, and pressed herself flat to the clapboard. Her heart stepped up a beat and shivery excitement moved through her loins as she twisted her head to peer into the room. A hitch came to her breath, and despite the chill, her palms dampened.

Bethany was stirring on the bed. Hell, she had told Drake that woman might come out of it. She had a reason to live, a strong one: she wanted to see her brother dead and had hired Laramie to do it. Revenge was as powerful a motivator to living as love, she reckoned.

She watched a few moments, until the young woman on the bed went still again, eyes closed, breathing even.

Asleep again. She hadn't quite come out of it but she would, given another day or two.

She wouldn't have *one* day, if Lily

had anything to say about it.

She pressed her hands to the glass, pushed upward. The window came up an inch and she switched her grip to the wooden base, lifted in fractional increments. She hoped the sawbones was in bed by now, since the rest of the place was dark, and wouldn't hear the slight sounds she made raising the window and climbing into the room.

The window was a bit high off the ground, but not high enough to stop her from pulling herself up and swinging a leg over the sill. She was strong for a girl, had to be, the way some of her marks got rough sometimes. She hoisted herself through the opening, high-laced shoes touching the floor inside with barely a sound.

Once inside, she stood still a moment in the low-turned lantern light, studying the young woman she had come to kill. What the hell did a man like Drake Lewis or John Laramie see in such a woman, anyway? She wasn't that pretty; more plain than anything else. She likely didn't know the things Lily knew when it came to pleasing their menfolk. She was a dish-rag, weak in many ways, stupid in others. She didn't deserve to survive on her own. Only the strong did. Like herself. Only those who took what they needed from others beneath them. Lily had learned that long ago.

Bethany Lewis was a rabbit and Lily was her hawk. She giggled again, unable to stop herself. She enjoyed the feeling of power she had over the helpless. Drake Lewis would see that at first hand later tonight.

The thought of his face when she told him his sister was dead gave her another giggle but she quickly stifled it as Bethany stirred again. Lily froze, waited. She preferred Bethany did not open her eyes, let out a warning scream that would wake the sawbones. But it didn't matter, because the result would be the same.

Lily's gaze swept about the room, stopped at a hardbacked chair that held a pillow. She smiled, the fever in her blood burning hotter.

'Such a poor little thing,' she whispered, as she went to the chair and lifted the pillow. 'Let Lily put you out of your misery. You just don't deserve to live, Sugar . . . '

She went to the bed, peered down at Bethany, contempt flowing into her eyes. She pressed the pillow over the young woman's face.

Bethany suddenly struggled, apparently border-line conscious, a weak pathetic effort. Lily jammed the pillow down harder, teeth gritting, a reflection of evil twisting her features.

'No, no, dear,' she said, through the gritted teeth. 'Don't make it any harder than it has to be. Let the darkness take you.'

Bethany Lewis's struggling began to cease. Lily let out a satisfied laugh.

The bedroom door suddenly came open and Lily's head whirled.

'What the hell's going on here?' the sawbones yelled, startled to see Lily bent over the young woman.

'Dammit, Doc,' Lily said, releasing the pillow. 'You got the worst timin'.'

The doctor stepped into the room, came straight at her. That was his first mistake — and his last.

Lily's hand dipped into the top of her blouse, then came back out with a two-shot derringer. She pulled the trigger twice.

The sawbones stopped in mid-stride, mouth coming open. He looked down at the two holes in his nightshirt, a crimson orchid blooming around each. Blood trickled from his lips and he dropped to his knees, then fell forward face first.

Lily peered at him, waiting for his last gurgling breath. She enjoyed such things. Tremendously. And when the death rattle came she wasn't disappointed.

She turned her attention back to the bed, grabbed the pillow again.

'Don't you just hate it when somebody interrupts you when you're right in the middle of something?' she muttered, a lilt in her voice as death made her giddy. 'Now . . . where were we?'

11

John Laramie reined to a halt a half mile from Black Hill, moonlight making his face look like something carved from stone. His hands tightened on the reins, bleaching, tendons rippling.

You will have to kill him.

He would have a choice to make: bring Drake Lewis in for hanging or shoot it out. A man like that would not come peaceably, so he reckoned the latter was the greater possibility. He'd been forced into killing bandits too many times to delude himself. But it wasn't the killings in self-defense that plagued his nightmares. It was the times he knew he could have taken those men alive, but had chosen not to. Those times he had known they would escape the hangman's noose, despite the fact they had all been cold-blooded killers. Fancy lawyers in frock-coats got some of them off, while others walked because of lack of evidence. He'd seen it too many times to rely on the fickle ways of the system.

So he had shot them. Pretended to give them a chance by letting them go for their guns and rationalized it as necessary.

But not this time. This time, if he killed Drake Lewis in true self-defense, he could walk away from the darkness inside him with a clear conscience. As long as he didn't play judge, jury and executioner, he would be a free man and if Bethany survived, perhaps a content one.

Of course, there was a third option, he reckoned. Drake Lewis hadn't stayed alive this long because of pure meanness. He had cunning, skill. And John Laramie might draw the short stick and wind up with a bullet in his heart this time.

He took a deep breath of chilled night air, eased out of the saddle. After tethering his bay to a cottonwood branch, he scooted forward, angling to the left of the trail as he made his way towards the side of the hill. Taking Lewis by surprise likely was not going to be easy, especially if the outlaw had any more men. There might be lookouts.

He went onward, seeking to make as little noise as possible but frosted-coated dead leaves occasionally crackled beneath his boots, or he stepped on a brittle twig that seemed to snap as loud as a gunshot in the silence. A few hundred yards on he spotted the cabin on the old mining grounds. Ten years ago a silver mine had thrived here, before the bottom fell out of the silver market and likely the mine had dried up. A number such mines peppered the area. Cabins had been abandoned along with the mines, providing perfect hideouts for outlaws and squatters.

Light seeped from inside the cabin, falling across the ground in a serrated pattern. He noted a horse tethered to a post at the far side of the place. As his gaze scanned the grounds he failed to pick out any signs of lookouts, but stands of pine, birch and cottonwood provided more than enough concealment for anyone hiding.

A heartbeat later the hairs on the back of his neck tingled as his manhunter's sixth sense kicked in. Although he saw nothing suspicious, an alarm went off in his mind just the same. His hand drifted to the Peacemaker's grip, lingered there, feeling its comforting solidness for a five count, before drawing. He lifted the gun to the side of his face, moved forward again, keeping to shadows and drifting from tree to tree to prevent any possible lurker from getting a clear target.

The cabin had a short porch, three steps leading up to it. There was a window to the side, and one at the front. He angled to the side, pressed close to the log wall and chanced a look inside. Bedrolls and a small table with cards scattered upon it met his gaze, but no sign of Drake Lewis.

His manhunter's sixth sense suddenly shot up a notch, but it was too late to do anything about it.

Something crashed into the side of his skull. He tried to jerk his head sideways at the last second, avoid the brunt of the blow, was only partially successful. Stars exploded before his eyes and his gun dropped from numbed fingers.

Through the roar in his head he heard a sharp laugh, then glimpsed a deeper darkness against the night sweeping towards him. An arm, holding a gun.

He tried to fall back, escape the blow but it took him across the jaw, sending pain ringing through his teeth.

The ground came up to meet him as his knees buckled. His face slammed into the hardpack and through a dark haze that threatened to completely overtake his consciousness, he sensed someone bending over him, grabbing him beneath the arms and dragging him along the ground. His limbs refused to work, offer any resistance. Boots clomped as he was hoisted up the steps. The figure dropped him a moment, opened the door then pulled him inside the cabin, kicking the door shut behind them.

Lantern glow highlighted his captor's duster, and gleamed from slicked-back hair the color of coal. Drake Lewis, if Laramie had to guess. Lewis lifted Laramie into a chair at the small table, then took the one opposite. He set a fist on the table, one holding a Smith & Wesson aimed at the manhunter, and waited.

A ringing set up in Laramie's skull and he was conscious of blood running down the side of his head. The use of his limbs started to return and he shook his head to clear his vision, a mistake as the ringing turned into a pounding.

'Lewis,' he said, voice low, hand going to the side of his head, feeling wetness there. He pulled back his fingers to see them slick with crimson, wiped it on his denim shirt.

'I ain't one of your common owlhoots, Laramie,' Drake Lewis said, voice damning. 'My men should have been back by now. It was a simple kill. That they ain't ... well, figured I wouldn't sit around waiting for someone to come put a bullet in me.'

Laramie shifted forward a bit, planting his feet solidly on the floorboards beneath the table.

'Don't get fidgety, Laramie. You'll get a couple extra minutes to live if you sit still.'

'Why didn't you just kill me?' Laramie's tone came defiant. He refused to fear this man the way the townsfolk had.

Lewis shrugged. 'When I make a kill I like to be lookin' in a man's eyes. I like to watch him beg, cower in fear.'

'You picked the wrong guy.' Laramie's gaze didn't waver, held the outlaw's.

Lewis's brows arched. 'I concede that. You ain't a man to fear anyone, are you?' The outlaw paused, as if studying him. 'But you fear something, don't you? All men do. Whether it's losing their loved ones like that useless marshal in town or the loss of their dignity, like my sister.'

''Cept her dignity's intact, despite what you did to her.'

A grim expression came to the outlaw's face. 'She's more than I bargained for. She set you on me?'

Laramie nodded. 'Had no idea who you were before I came in here. Heard stories about your gang, but I didn't come lookin' for you.'

Lewis shifted the gun slightly, aiming it directly at Laramie's heart. 'Marshal dead?'

'He went out with his dignity intact, too.'

'Stupid fool. Who'd a thought he'd grow some balls at the end. My men dead, too?'

Laramie cocked his head, spat a stream of blood and saliva at the floor. 'Reckon they will be once the law comes for them.'

Drake Lewis let a snake of a smile slither over his lips. 'See, that's where you're wrong, Laramie. Only ones alive in this town who know me and might connect me to killin's is you, the barkeep, Lily . . . and my sister. I'll be payin' the 'keep and Lily a visit later. My sister, well, she might never wake up and you . . . you won't be telling anybody.'

Laramie's eyes narrowed. 'Then kill me now, Lewis.'

The outlaw peered at him a long moment, as if puzzled by the manhunter's utter lack of fear. Then he began to laugh, though the gun did not waver in its aim on Laramie's chest.

'I see it now, Laramie. Indeed, I do. You got the same darkness in you as I got in me. Only yours is waitin' on you. Mine . . . mine done took me the day I was born.'

'We're nothing alike, Lewis. And you made a mistake not killin' me outside. Same one all your kind make.'

Lewis thumbed back the hammer on

his gun. 'And what might that be, Laramie?'

'You all get cocky, full of yourselves.' Laramie's legs came off the floor then. He brought them up with explosive force, knees connecting with the underneath of the table and hurling it upwards. Cards fluttered to the floor.

Lewis's gun blasted as the outlaw reflexively jerked the trigger. The bullet punched through the wooden table top but wide of Laramie, whose feet hit the ground and propelled him out of the chair.

The recoil took the gun out of Lewis's hand, sent it tumbling through the air to land on the floor near one of the bedrolls. Lewis appeared momentarily stunned at the lack of a weapon in his hand and Laramie flung the table, which had landed on edge, aside. He hurled himself at Lewis, snapping a short jab into the outlaw's face.

Unable to plant his feet, he didn't get a lot of force behind the blow and Lewis shook it off. The outlaw grabbed two handfuls of Laramie's shirt, whirled him around and flung him into a log wall.

The manhunter hit hard, the impact rattling his spine and sending shocks of jagged light across his vision.

Lewis moved in, launching a punch that would have taken Laramie's head off. The manhunter ducked, catching only a glancing blow. The outlaw's fist slammed into the log wall with a brittle snap of sound.

'Jesus!' the outlaw yelled, drawing back his hand. Blood flowed over his mangled knuckles. Laramie reckoned at least two had been broken beyond repair; Lewis would not have full use of that hand again.

He gave it little thought. He slammed Lewis with a right cross that sent the outlaw staggering.

Heart pounding, breath beating out, Laramie swung again and again. Rage seared through his veins.

Kill him! Do it, Laramie. Make him pay for what he did to Bethany!

Each blow connected, snapping Lewis's head back and forth like it was on a coach spring. Blood sprayed from Lewis's nose and lips, both of which were mashed to a pulp. Still Laramie swung, a crimson haze coating his vision, every single ounce of fury over Bethany Lewis lying in that bed gutshot surging free.

Lewis somehow managed to stay on his feet. The man was used to beatings, had been ever since he was a child. He took each hit silently, refusing to go down or cry out.

And John Laramie was just as glad. The darkness inside him surged up, drinking in that fury, embracing it, driving it harder.

At last Lewis collapsed, his legs giving out. He sank to his knees, body wavering, one eye swelling shut, face a mask of scarlet.

Laramie hit him again, knocking the outlaw over backward. Lewis twisted, tried to crawl along the floor, towards his gun, but Laramie kicked him in the ribs, hurling him over on to his back.

Gasping, blood bubbling from his lips, the hardcase lay still. Laramie was gasping as well, readying himself for a kick at the man's unprotected head, a blow that would end his life.

Do it, Laramie! You know you want to. If you take him in he might escape a noose. You can't let that happen. Kill him now!

Laramie shook his head, Bethany's face flashing through his mind. If he killed Lewis, there would be no chance for them, no possible future together. The darkness would win and he would return to the trail, a killing machine, unredeemable.

No! No, he would not kill him.

He stepped back, fighting to catch his breath, sweat and blood streaming down his face, the outlaw's blood coating his fists.

No, he would not kill him. He would bring him in. If — *when* Bethany regained consciousness, she could testify against her brother. The coward barkeep or Lily sure as hell wouldn't.

But Bethany had found her courage. She would take the stand and Drake would hang — once he persuaded her not to kill him.

He bent, plucked the Bowie knife from the outlaw's boot and stuck it inside his own.

Muscles in his legs and arms trembling, he backed away, retrieved Lewis's gun, then popped the gate and let the bullets clatter to the floor. He went to the door, opened it and hurled the gun out into the night.

He cast a backward glance at Lewis. The outlaw was breathing in ragged gasps. He wasn't going anywhere for the moment.

As he stepped out into the night the chilled air splashed his face and his heart started to slow. The darkness. He had beaten it. There was still a chance for the man named John Laramie, and maybe that chance would be with Bethany.

Body aching, he went down the steps and to the side of the house. It took him only a moment to locate his own gun, which he shoved back into its holster.

Returning to the front, he went to Lewis's horse, grabbed a coil of rope attached to the saddle. He went back into the cabin, tossed it beside the outlaw, then knelt and turned Lewis on to his belly. He drew the Bowie knife from his boot, cut lengths of rope, then bound the outlaw's wrists and ankles.

After returning the knife to his boot, he grabbed Lewis's ankles and dragged him outside, being none too careful as he pulled him down the three steps. He left him on the ground while he went back to the horse and untethered the reins, then led it to Lewis.

Lewis's eye opened — Laramie couldn't tell whether the other one would have because it had swollen completely shut.

'What . . . ' Lewis said, words liquidly.

'Takin' you to see your sister, Lewis. I made her a promise. You best hope she's awake by now. Then you're going to join your men in the marshal's jail.'

Laramie stooped, hoisted Lewis up and laid him across the saddle. He grabbed the reins, led the horse towards the trail. When he reached his own horse, he untethered the reins. Moments later, he climbed into the saddle after hitching a rope to Lewis's mount's saddle horn. He guided the second horse along the trail, praying Bethany Lewis had regained consciousness by now and would know he had kept his word.

12

John Laramie rode in silence. Nearing the sawbones's place fifteen minutes later, he glanced over at Drake Lewis, who had uttered only an occasional groan as his horse jounced along the trail. It was over. Lewis would not kill another man nor rape another woman. And the darkness John Laramie had felt struggling to take control was now a thing of the past, he assured himself.

But all that didn't matter for the moment. Only one thing weighed on his mind: the fate of the young woman fighting for her life at the doc's.

He reckoned it was funny how quickly priorities could change. In the space of two days he'd gone from a man wanting to be left to his own to a man wanting to find out what life had to offer with another.

Whether she would feel the same, he

didn't know. But it was worth seeing it through.

He guided the horses towards the hitch rail at the front of the office, reined up. Every inch of his body ached as he climbed from the saddle, and tethered his mount to the rail. He went around to Lewis's horse and did the same. He paused before the outlaw, took the man's chin between a thumb and forefinger, lifted it so he could look into the outlaw's good eye.

'Don't go anywhere, you hear?' he said, then let the man's chin drop back down. Lewis muttered an obscenity.

'Might say the same to you, Laramie.' A voice sounded from the side of the house. His gaze went in that direction. The redheaded bar dove had stepped around the corner, holding a derringer in both hands, aiming at his head.

He cursed himself for getting complacent. He had forgotten about the girl, but had figured she would be in town, waiting on Lewis. That she wasn't . . .

No.

A sinking sensation hit his belly as a vicious smile took hold of the girl's thin lips. 'Why don't you just go ahead an' cut him loose, manhunter.'

'What have you done?' Laramie's voice came cold and something inside him turned to ice.

Lily giggled. Insanity laced the sound. 'Why, I done Drake there a big ol' favor, I reckon. After all, couldn't have witnesses givin' out his name to every which lawdog that rode in here, right, Drake honey?'

Drake Lewis's head lifted, a guttural sound came from between his swollen lips. 'I'll kill you,' he said, voice hoarse.

Lily let out another sharp giggle. 'Oh, no you won't, Drake darlin', 'cause I aim to kill you first.' Her gaze shifted back to Laramie. 'Unbuckle your gunbelt and kick it over here.' She came a few steps closer, her aim unwavering from his head.

That was good. The head was a more difficult target than the body and it was a small gun, though it could damn well kill him as fast as any Colt. But he didn't care. He knew with chilled certainty what had happened and why this girl was standing out here threatening them. And even if she shot him he was going to take her down.

His hand swept downward without thought. Lily did not expect him to draw. She never fired.

But John Laramie did.

The Peacemaker came up in a blur. The shot sounded unnaturally loud in the chilled night, echoed through the frosty air like demons laughing.

Lily jolted as a bullet punched into her chest. She stood there a moment, looked down at the round hole in her blouse and the scarlet stain spreading around it. She staggered a step, looked back to him, derringer still held straight out. She pulled the trigger twice. Empty clacks sounded.

She giggled. 'Bang — bang,' she said, then fell forward and hit the ground face first.

Laramie wasted no time checking whether she were dead. He knew she was, and though the gun had been empty it was still self-defense, for all that that mattered, now.

The front door was locked and his leg snapped out, bootheel slamming into the wood. The door burst inward with a resounding shudder, the jamb splintering about the lock. He plunged through the waiting area, then the examination room. The door leading to the back room was open, light spilling from within.

He halted as he reached it, spotting the doctor's body on the floor. A glance told him the sawbones was dead.

As his gaze lifted to the bed, he swore that in that moment his heart stopped beating. And never started again.

He went to her, stood beside the bed, looking down, a sensation of utter helplessness washing over him. Her hand hung over the edge of the bed, pale, lifeless. He took it in his own. Cold, so cold. So . . .

Dead.

'No!' he yelled, shaking his head, tears flooding his eyes but not falling. 'Please, no . . . ' His voice dropped to a whisper, then nothingness.

She was gone. And though he had killed her murderer, he felt no sense of satisfaction or justice. He would have let the dove and Lewis both go if somehow he could bring Bethany Lewis back to life. But he couldn't. After all, he was just a man. One who was too late. Again. And would live whatever was left of his life knowing it.

He gently set her hand on the bed, swallowed hard at the emotion balling in his throat. He pulled the blanket up over her head, the coldness surging back into his innards.

After a moment, he went back outside and stood on the porch, frozen in grief and black thought for long moments. At last, he glanced at the bargirl lying dead on the cold ground, then at Drake Lewis, whose head came up.

'She's gone . . . ' the outlaw said, no emotion in his tone.

Laramie nodded. 'She's gone.'

He knew what came with the outlaw's question. No sense of guilt, remorse or loss, no grief for a young woman he had wronged. Just relief. Because now no one was left to testify against him, except the manhunter himself. That might be enough; it might not. Laramie couldn't directly tie him to a murder. His men had killed the marshal. The man who had shot Bethany was dead. The barkeep might be coerced into talking, but what could he know? That Lewis had come to town, threatened them? So what?

No, Lewis wouldn't hang. He might even get off with the help of some fancy lawyer.

A choice. Again. Between the darkness inside and riding off into retirement, letting the law possibly set this man free. To kill and rape and rob. To terrorize and seek revenge.

A choice? No, no choice. Not

210

anymore. There was nothing ahead for the man named John Laramie. Nothing but living out his days with guilt and nightmares.

He took slow deliberate steps down the stairs to the ground. There, he stooped, pulling the Bowie knife from his boot, then went to the horse holding the outlaw.

'You were right, Lewis, about the darkness inside me wanting to make me like you. I've been fighting it for years now. Your type put it in me. Thought I could escape it but like your sister told me, gotta face my demons instead of running away from them.' He sliced through the rope holding the outlaw's ankles, then went around to the opposite side and cut through the ones binding his wrists.

Drake Lewis didn't move. He stared at John Laramie with his one good eye. 'You're duty bound to bring me in, Laramie. I surrender.'

Laramie uttered a lifeless laugh. 'The man who thrived on the fear of others . . . now, the man who knows fear himself.' It was there, on the outlaw's face: fear, the gleaming skull of his approaching death. Like all those who terrified others, a coward at the end.

Laramie thrust Lewis off the horse. The outlaw hit the ground on his side, groaned.

Then, after walking around to his own horse, Laramie opened a saddlebag and pulled out his spare gun. He tossed it on the ground a few feet from Drake Lewis.

'The hell . . . ' Lewis muttered, voice no longer steady.

'Givin' you a sporting chance, Lewis. Go for the gun. Kill me . . . if you can.'

'There's no chance,' Lewis muttered.

'More chance than you gave any of your victims.'

Drake Lewis's mouth tightened with spite. His open eye flicked toward the gun lying a few feet away. He was a dead man and he knew it, but driven by the black force of his own corruption and cowardice, the same as any outlaw in the end. With a sudden lunge, he grabbed for the weapon.

Kill him!

Laramie waited for Drake Lewis to touch the ivory handle, then his hand swept to his Peacemaker.

For a heartbeat, the crash of thunder filled the night, an instant later accompanied by the laughing echoes of the gun blast that soon faded into the night's darkness.

Lewis had grasped the gun, managed to swing it around and up, just as lead punched into his forehead. The outlaw's head snapped back and his lifeless body settled on the frosty ground.

Laramie holstered his Peacemaker, wondering if the chilled numbness that pervaded his being would ever leave. He doubted it. Not without the warmth that that woman lying dead inside the back room might have provided for him. She was the balance he had sought and at the end his demons had won. He belonged to the darkness, now.

And God help the guilty.

We do hope that you have enjoyed reading this large print book.

Did you know that all of our titles are available for purchase?

We publish a wide range of high quality large print books including:
Romances, Mysteries, Classics
General Fiction
Non Fiction and Westerns

Special interest titles available in large print are:
The Little Oxford Dictionary
Music Book, Song Book
Hymn Book, Service Book

Also available from us courtesy of Oxford University Press:
Young Readers' Dictionary
(large print edition)
Young Readers' Thesaurus
(large print edition)

For further information or a free brochure, please contact us at:
Ulverscroft Large Print Books Ltd.,
The Green, Bradgate Road, Anstey,
Leicester, LE7 7FU, England.
Tel: (00 44) 0116 236 4325
Fax: (00 44) 0116 234 0205

Other titles in the
Linford Western Library:

WHEN LIGHTNING STRIKES

Ethan Flagg

Lightning Cal Gentry's reputation as a lethal gunfighter has its downsides: he faces hotheads making their play, and hardcases who want respect and fame. It's hard to remain at the top — and now Cal wants out. But when he guns down Billy Vance in the New Mexico town of Tucumcari, it prompts a manhunt, putting his loved ones in mortal danger. Only with the help of the infamous renegade Apache, Geronimo, can he hope to resolve the issue.

SHOWDOWN IN JEOPARDY

John Davage

Near Cutler's Pass, a derailed train is raided for its $80,000 gold shipment . . . Five years later in the town of Jeopardy, Clyde Pascoe is shot and killed by an unknown assassin. Sheriff Cyrus Yapp and newspaper editor Will Bullard link Pascoe's death with the Cutler's Pass train raid. They suspect that a newcomer to Jeopardy, Luke Frey, is involved in the murders suddenly occurring in Jeopardy . . . whilst Luke's interest lies in discovering the identity of the train's mysterious fifth raider . . .